Knox

ERIKSON BROTHERS BOOK 5

KATHI S. BARTON

This is a work of fiction. Names, characters, places, and incidents are products of the author's imagination or are used fictitiously and are not to be construed as real. Any resemblance to actual events, locations, organizations, or persons, living or dead, is entirely coincidental.

World Castle Publishing, LLC
Pensacola, Florida

Copyright © 2025 Kathi S. Barton
Hardback ISBN: 9798277220368
Paperback ISBN: 9798891264984
eBook ISBN: 9798891264991
First Edition World Castle Publishing, LLC, December 22, 2025
http://www.worldcastlepublishing.com

Licensing Notes

Cover: Cover Designs by Karen
Editor: Karen Fuller

Chapter 1

Knox didn't understand the paperwork in front of him. Actually, he wasn't sure if it was the paperwork or if he was just having a bad day. It had started out all right, but as soon as noon rolled around, he was having shit happen that had him pissed off at the world. Things just weren't going the way that he'd hoped when he left his house this morning.

Focusing on the paperwork now that he'd gotten something for his headache, he knew two things at once. He needed more research on the wording of the thing, and that the trial coming up for Carrie was going to be a bust if he didn't get someone to tell him where all her family was living. Blowing out of his mouth, he sat back in his chair and closed his eyes for a moment. He really did need to think about something else other than Carrie and her upcoming trial against her family.

Carrie Sharp had five brothers and three sisters who all wanted the same thing from her. Their mother's social security checks that came to her monthly. Not one of them had a job, nor did they feel the need to get one, so long as there was money around that they could steal. However, because their mother was staying in a nursing home now, the checks went to them instead of Carrie. Not that Carrie used it for anything but her mother, but they thought it was free cash so long as they got to her before one of the others did.

They weren't above beating her up for the money either. Leaving her to have to work three jobs so that she could afford her mother's meds and food on the table, before his family stepped in. Carrie had been beaten so badly before that she'd been injured in a way that made it so that she couldn't have kids. His heart hurt for the younger woman, and he wanted to make things right for her in this world. And his job was to do the research for the upcoming trial of her against her brothers and sisters.

"I have a question for you." He smiled at Carrie and told her that he was just thinking about her when he showed up at his office. "I hope in a good way. I know this is costing you a fortune in keeping me hiding out in a hotel until you find them all. I have to say it's been kind of nice having someone clean up after me. But to have someone make the bed is the best. I hate making my bed in the morning."

"I don't care for it either. It's why there are times when I want to get myself a sleeping bag so that I can sleep in it and just straighten it out in the morning before I leave for work." He asked her what her question was. "Not that I mind looking for them, but I have a couple of questions about your family as well. Like, where are they?"

"They are living in the old house that my parents were renting. I don't believe that they're paying any rent there, but they are staying there. I think that Allen keeps the owner at bay most of the time. He's the meanest of them all." He made notes on what she was telling him. "He's scary dangerous to be around. He'd kill you with his bare hands with witnesses and claim that you were setting him up. I avoid him most of all. My question is, do you know how much longer I'm going to be staying at the hotel? While it's nice and all, I'm bored out of my mind staying there."

"As soon as they're all arrested, then you can be free to move around." He told her all, but Allen and Syble had been arrested so far, and they were all in the cells at the new jail. "I'm looking for them both, but they're being tricky about things. I'll have the police go to the old homestead to see what they can figure out. Thanks for that."

"No worries. I was just wondering." She sat down, and he waited for her to speak again. "I'm going to owe you all my life if things don't change up soon for me. As it stands right now, I think that I'm going to be paying you back until well beyond my retirement years."

"You've been told you don't have to worry

about paying it back, correct? All we want you to do is to pay it forward when you have a chance. That way, you can help someone else out when they need it. I like that better than you thinking that you're going to be beholden to us forever." She told him that she doubted very much anyone would need as much help as she'd needed. "You'd be surprised. There are a lot of people out there in need of a hand up. And you're going to be in the position to help them out sometime."

"I hope so." He felt better about doing the work now, and he was glad that she'd stopped by. She made him feel good about himself, and he was forever grateful for her input on things, too. She was smart. "All right, I'll let you get back to whatever you were doing. I have another program that I'm working on and needed a short break from it to clear my head."

"I was having the same trouble. I'm glad that you stopped by." He picked up the next file that was on his desk when she left and decided that he needed to change up what he was doing. This one was the file on his brother, Demi and Mandy adopting her nephews now that they were married. It was going to be good for all four of them when things were settled, and he couldn't have been happier for them. He answered his cell phone without looking to see who it might be. It was his brother Dusty.

"I have two investments that I think you'll want

to get in on the bottom floor with." He told him that he was in. "Just like that? You don't even want to know the details?"

"I trust you more with my money than I do myself at times." He thought of when Alex, Locke's wife, had gone over his books and found a great deal of money they were all paying out for things that they didn't need. Like Locke was paying for a service to come in and press his suits monthly when he didn't wear them but once or twice a year. There were things like cable bills, too, that they were paying for that didn't even come close to being right. One of them had been paying for the cable bill at the local bar that would order the big fights and other things and charged it to his account. She'd saved them a great deal of money by going over their books, and he was very careful now to look over his billing monthly and to sign his own checks. They'd been taken advantage of by their accountants as well. It was a nightmare to get fixed, but she'd done it all for them.

"It'll be long-term, just so you know, but the profits will be epic when they're ready. I can get us both in on the ground floor today if you want to invest." He told him how much he wanted to invest in the venture, and Dusty thought that was a good amount. "Good. Now I'll be giving you the paperwork in the morning so that you have it when you need it."

"Thanks. I'll look forward to going over it." Not that he would really. He trusted his brothers with everything that he had. Especially his love. He loved them all so much that he wondered at times if there were words strong enough to tell someone how he actually felt about them. "We're still on for dinner, right? I know that Shipley has that thing tonight with the other women in the family."

"Yeah, I've made us reservations at the restaurant in Coshocton. We're to be there at six. I hope that's all right with everyone." He said he was sure that it would be and thanked him again for doing that. "I love eating at the Warehouse. They have the best steaks around and don't get me started on their onion rings."

"Now I'm hungry." They both laughed and then closed their phones. He really was hungry now and decided to go find something to eat to tide him over. It was only one o'clock right now, so he'd eat something light to make sure he didn't get a headache from that too. His cook was making bread when he entered the room. "I'm sorry. I thought I told you that I'd be going out tonight."

"You did, sir. I'm making bread for the stew that I'm making for tomorrow. It's an overnight kind of bread, and I'm excited to see how it turns out. If nothing else, you'll have biscuits with your stew." He told her that he'd enjoy it either way. "You're easy to please. You need a wife around to keep you on your toes. Like your other brothers."

"I don't know that there is anyone out there for me." He thought of Carrie and smiled at the thought of having her as his wife. "Carrie would be busting my chops over every little thing. She's hard on people, I think. But a good person."

"Now, there is a woman that you need in your life. She's a good person and has had a lot going on with her to make her sour, but she's not. You'd do well to have someone like her in your life." He said they were just friends. "I see the way you two look at one another. Like you're in love but too stubborn to admit it. You and she? Well, I can see you two having the best marriage of all of your family. You have her as your friend first, and that's always a good thing."

"Nah, we're just good friends." He smiled at the thought of them being together and nearly laughed. "She's not my type. She's more Zander's type. I think of her as a little sister more than someone that I would even date."

"Mark my words, she'll be good for you. Get you out of the house, too." He would admit that he'd been spending too much time in the house of late. It seemed to be too cold out to do much more than run to the mailbox for the mail and back in the house. He'd even been working from home a lot more because he didn't want to deal with people. Not that he hated people, but he would rather be alone than anything else. His cell was ringing when he got back to his office after having a sandwich of bologna and cheese.

"He's here." He knew the whispered voice, and he was suddenly terrified for Carrie. "He's at the desk in the lobby of the hotel I'm staying at, giving them a hard time about not allowing him to know if I'm here or not."

"I'm on my way. Where are you?" She told him how one of the clerks had met her at the front door to tell her not to go in. "Good for them. Stay put, and I'll be there in about twenty minutes."

He was never so grateful to catch all the green lights as he'd been today. He called the police as soon as he got into his car. As soon as he pulled up in front of the hotel, she got into his car and told him to drive. He was more than happy to do that for her and made his way down to the next block just as she noticed that Syble was walking down the street too.

"We'll get them both now, and then we can start the process of a hearing. I have everything that I need to get them put in jail for the rest of their lives." She asked about her mother. "She'll be fine where she is. I just hope that once these two are off the streets, things will go better for you now."

"I'd like that." She watched as her sister stopped people on the streets, no doubt asking if they'd seen her. "It would be easier on them if they had a job for all the work they put into not having to work, I'd think. What exactly are we having them arrested for? I meant to ask you that before, but I was just so happy that someone was getting them out of my hair that I forgot."

"Forgery is the biggest one. They signed the back of your mother's government check when it came in before you could get to it." She asked him if there was anything else. "Yes. Mostly, it's petty stuff that will have them serving jail time, but the biggest one is, like I said, forgery. Not to mention stealing from their own mother and you so that you couldn't take care that she had what she needed."

"I'm so grateful to have them off the streets that—look, there's the police." They watched as Syble was arrested. She would get resisting arrest, too, if he didn't miss his bet. The way that she was fighting with the officers who had her was enough to make him feel sorry for them. He was glad when she was handcuffed and put into the back of the cruiser. "She went a lot harder than I thought that she would. I wonder what she said to them. I can imagine that it wasn't all that nice."

Driving to park across the street from the hotel, they pulled up in time to see Allen being arrested as well. He looked a little bloodied and worse for wear, but he was in cuffs too and on his way to sitting in the back of the cruiser that had come for him. He'd never been so glad to see someone arrested as he was the two of them. He knew that he'd sleep better tonight just knowing that they were off the streets and in custody. Now all he had to worry about was if Zander would be able to use what he'd found about them to put them away for a while.

"I don't know how to thank you for this." He said it had been his pleasure, and it had been. "I can go back to my place and sleep better tonight. Just knowing that they're going to be going to jail for a little while makes me feel so much better."

"I understand that. It's been a long time in coming." It had only been about three weeks, but it felt like forever to him as well. "I can help you pack up if you want, and I'll take you home. You will still need to be careful until the trial. I don't see them getting out to cause more damage, but you never know about the judge that is coming through to hear the pretrial things that are set up about them."

"I'll be careful. I don't know that I know how to be anything but careful. Now I can go and visit my mom without worrying about them finding out where she was." He told her that he'd take her now if she wanted to go. "No, you've done enough for me today.

Just knowing that you were coming to get me made me feel so much better."

When she got out of the car and crossed the street, he thought about what Shirley had said to him just before he left. That Carrie would be good for him. He thought that he was doing all right for himself; he couldn't imagine what she was talking about. Going back to his home, he was sitting at his desk an hour later with no idea what he'd been thinking about or if he'd gotten anything done today. He needed a nap and a good run. Both of which he was going to do right now.

~*~

Demi was having fun with his brothers. They met up at least once a week to have a good meal together, and tonight was the night. As soon as Knox showed up, he told them that the other Jameson family had been arrested and were in jail. He said that Carrie was moving back to her old place even as he spoke.

"You didn't help her?" He said that he'd lent her his car to drive her things home, but she wouldn't hear of him trying to help her pack. "She'd be like that, too. I'm betting that if you hadn't given her your car, she would have toted things to her place on her own. She's stubborn like that."

"I know." He looked at his brother and wondered why he hadn't started dating Carrie. As far as he could see, they'd be a perfect match. They both liked their solitude and were smart. There were other things that they had in common, but right now, all he could see was that they were missing out on the best time of their lives, not being together. "What are you mumbling about?"

"I was just thinking that you and Carrie would make a good couple." He said he was the second person today to have said that to him. "Really? Who else can see you two together other than half the state?"

"My cook." He nodded, thinking that his brother wasn't seeing what they could all see. That they really would make a perfect couple. "I'm not going to date Carrie. She's like my little sister or something. I'm just glad that we have a good relationship like we have right now and not have to worry about dating and stuff like that."

"Maybe she needs to be with Zander. Did you think of that?" He said that she'd eat Zander alive; he was just too kind for someone as ballsy as Carrie was to date. "Ballsy? I don't see that. Now, Alex and even my wife included are ballsy, but not Carrie. She's too delicate."

"Really? That's what you see when you look at her? Christ man, have you met her family? And the very fact that she'd come out on top of them makes me think that she's stronger than even your wife and

Alex. Shipley might be a little more so than Carrie, but I see a strong woman who has put up with a lot with her family and still has a good outlook on things in her life. She's also very smart and good to have in your corner."

"Sounds like you do like her." Knox said that he did, but she wasn't his type. He didn't know what his type was, but he knew that Carrie wasn't it. "You're good friends too. That's always a plus. I think you should take her out and see what sort of stars line up for you."

"I don't want to date her. She isn't my type." When he sounded a little angry, Demi apologized to him. "It's all right. I'm sorry. It's just that I know that I don't want to date her, and having her pushed on me isn't something that I want either. She's a good friend, and I'd like for her to continue to be, so I don't want to mess it up by asking her to date me. Understand?"

"Yes, I do. And I'm sorry." Knox waved him off, but he still felt bad about making him angry. Deciding to change the subject, he told him how the breakfast thing was going at the school. And about the teachers returning on Monday.

A month ago, seventeen teachers were given a month off without pay. When asked for a list of things they might need for their classrooms for the end of the year, they'd gotten padded lists of things like pallets of water and microwaves. What a second-grade class would need with a microwave is what got them to look at the lists a little better. There were things like gift cards that they wanted to paint their rooms when they had just been painted. Also, one of them wanted a case of paper plates and plasticware to use in their room. The kids didn't eat in the room, so no one could figure that out. When it was established that they were ordering things for their own homes, the board of the school laid them off without pay for a month. He wondered if any of them would be returning starting Monday.

David Sheen, the school principal, wanted to fire them all, but since teachers were in short supply anyway, they decided the best course of action was to give them time to reflect on what they'd done. Demi didn't think it would do any of them any good, but he'd not been in charge. He just did the breakfast thing.

"I heard that was going great for the kids. And the pancake breakfast was by far their favorite. I don't know if I could cook that many pancakes for a bunch of kids or not. It must take you forever to get them all fed." He said it was easy once he got into a rhythm. "Still. You'd have to be really good at being in a rhythm for you to feed two hundred kids pancakes and sausage in an hour."

"I'm great." They both laughed about his joke,

and he was glad that he no longer seemed mad. "I have a lot of good help, too, and some of the parents are coming in to eat as well. We don't charge them for coming in, and I think that it benefits them as much as the kids. I was told that it was the first hot meal of the day that they'd get if not for me being in there cooking. And I don't mind doing it. I get to see my boys while I'm working."

Demi had adopted his wife, Mandy's nephews, when they'd been nearly killed by their father. As it was, he was in prison for the rest of his life, and not beating them daily when they'd been living at home. Samuel had killed their mother in a fit of rage and had asked the cops, when they showed up, if they'd turn their backs for him to murder the two kids as well. It didn't bode well for him when he confessed to killing Betsey, his wife, while standing over her with a ball bat, either.

They all talked over one another for the two hours they were there. He'd gotten a really good steak from the menu, and his brothers had done the same. It wasn't like they couldn't have it anytime they wanted, but it was nice that they could all get together and have a good meal once a week with just themselves. The women did the same thing, and he knew that they enjoyed it as much as he did.

They didn't discuss business when they were

together like this either. It was a time for them to catch up on what they'd been doing all week and to relax. The staff here was used to them and how they tipped, so they got great service when they were there. The Warehouse was one of his favorite places to eat, as Martha had taken them all there when he'd graduated from college.

Martha Grable had been the best mother-like figure they'd ever had when the van they were driving broke down in front of her house. She'd been kind to them, loving as well. She'd also taught them to be good men and how to invest their money. They'd nearly doubled their money with her help, and he missed her every day.

"I was thinking about the holidays this morning. I can't believe that Thanksgiving is nearly upon us. Remember some of the good times that we had with Martha? Those were the best." Locke brought up Christmas then and said how it had been the first time they'd celebrated the holiday since they'd been born. Zander nodded as he continued. "I remember sitting at her table, where everything was right there, and wondering where we were going to stash the food when there were leftovers. Dad would have had a fit to see us all sitting around a table that he didn't get to be the head of."

Dad had been an abusive bastard and a drunk. It

was nothing for him to beat them daily, even as grown men, and end up in the hospital. He'd look for reasons to beat on them or not. It didn't matter if they'd done anything wrong either. He was just a bastard looking for trouble all the time. When he'd been put in jail for trying to kill one of them one Saturday evening, they'd loaded up in the van that Locke had purchased and left town. Never once had they been back and were happier for it. He died some years later, all alone in the house, and not one of them cared.

After the bill was paid, Locke usually picked up the bill. They went to their separate cars and talked more. It was funny to him, really, that they were so close in living next to one another and yet they would get together like they'd not seen each other in a month. He really loved his family and was glad that they got along so well.

"Did I tell you I've bought some lottery tickets?" They all laughed and said that they had too. "The lottery winnings are huge this time. If we could win that again, I don't know what we'd do with it all. We're rich enough now as it is."

About twelve years ago, now, Locke had bought a winning lottery ticket. He played the same numbers every week in that it was their day of birth, and played twenty-three on the last number because two of them were born on the same date. He'd not only won the biggest jackpot the lottery had ever had, but he shared it with all six of them to make them all billionaires. And since meeting Martha, they'd more than doubled their winnings to this day. None of them had to work, but they all had jobs. No one suspected they had all that money, and they liked it that way. No one would come to them with their hands out.

"You thinking that you need to have more winnings?" They all teased Locke for him playing the lottery and asked him if he played the same numbers. He told them that he added his wife's birthday on the card when he played. "I guess I'm going to start playing too. It couldn't hurt."

After they started leaving one car at a time, he and Knox were the only ones left. He asked him if he was still sore at him for talking about Carrie. He shook his head and told him how much he loved him. He couldn't have loved his brother more than he did at that moment, he thought.

"I'm not mad. I shouldn't have been so snappish to you either. I just don't like her in that way." He said that he understood. "I hope so. I do like her. I might even love her a little, but not like you love your wife. Carrie really does remind me of a little sister if we had one. But there is nothing romantic going on between us. I swear to you there isn't."

"I believe you. I didn't before, but I do now."

He nodded and opened his car door. Before getting in, Knox looked at him with an odd smile. "What? Are you going to tell me that you've found someone else that you love? Do you know how much I would cheer you on if you do?"

"I don't think there's anyone out there for me. I'm like an old man, set in my ways." He said that he wasn't. "It's Friday night, and I'm spending the evening with my married brothers. How much more old man is that? And right now, all I can think about is going home, changing into something more comfy, and sitting in my chair to read the newspaper that came before I left tonight. I'm old before my time, Demi, and I think I like that about me best of all."

On the way home, all he could think about was what his brother had told him. Old before his time. He might well have thought that too if Mandy hadn't come into his life before she had. He was working too hard at his own restaurant and snapping at everyone who got within a foot of him, simply because he had nothing to keep him at home. He was close to having a heart attack if not for his brother making him close down the place for a week so that he could rest. He'd not rested, but he had got to know Mandy and the boys a good deal better, and that had been the turning point in his life.

Pulling into his driveway, he was excited to be

home. He had a wonderful wife and two sons that he adored. Tomorrow, they were going to watch a football game together and pig out on snacks and soda. It was the best way that he could think of to spend a Saturday afternoon. Just hanging out with his family.

Going into the house, he was greeted with hello's and glad you're home. He'd only been gone for a few hours, but it had been long enough for them to have missed him. Being missed was almost as good as being loved, he thought. There was so much to both of them that he knew that he'd love them until the end of time and beyond. They were his everything.

Chapter 2

Elaine pulled into town about midnight and was exhausted. She'd heard that there were teaching positions open, and she was going to try her hardest to get one of them. She'd heard the scandal about the teachers padding their list and thought that they'd have to be stupid to think that no one would notice. However, she'd also heard of the Ericksons and wondered what sort of people they'd be to be able to afford to help the school out when they needed funding. She would like to get a little funding herself, but would wait for a job to come to her. As it was right now, she was sleeping in her car until she was able to find herself a place to live—if she got the job. If not, there were other positions open for teachers, and she'd try her best to get one of those if things didn't work out here.

"You can't park here." Smiling at the officer who was only doing his job, she said that she was just going to get a newspaper. "Oh well, that's all right then. Go on ahead. I think that they're tomorrow's paper, as I just saw Windell loading up the boxes on the other street. If you want to know anything about a job, you just ask me. I'll tell you what I know."

"Thank you. I was hearing about a teaching position that might be available around here." He said that he knew of three of them. "Oh. So many. I had heard there was some trouble. I didn't realize that three teachers had lost their jobs over it."

"Nah, they just got them better-paying jobs in the city and didn't want to quit while they'd been off. It's fine by me. My grandkids go to school there, and he said that the three of them weren't so nice anyway. What grade are you thinking of teaching? I think that kindergarten, third, and fourth are the ones that haven't been filled yet."

"I can teach kindergarten through high school. Also, some college classes. But I'm looking for something in a quiet town so that I can have some peace and quiet." He told her that they had plenty of that around here. "Good. Are the interviews still going on at the principal's office every morning? I believe that the newspaper said that it was first-come, first-served."

"That's right. There have only been a couple of people who have shown up to take on the jobs, so you might well be first if you can get there by eight when they start." She said she just needed a place to park. "You're not living out of your car, are you, miss? That's against the law."

"Just to sleep. It's too late to get into one of the bed and breakfasts around here." Not to mention, she didn't have the money for one of them. She'd been down to her last couple of bucks now for a while now. "I just need to rest up before tomorrow. It's been a long drive. Then I'll look for something more permanent tomorrow."

If she got the job. She had money enough to put a deposit down on something like a furnished apartment, but not much else. She'd be dipping into that over the next week if she didn't find herself a job that she could work at until she got to the next town on her list. Things had been rough for a few months now. Ever since she'd gotten out of the service.

When she said she was retiring, they suddenly lost her last three checks. She'd been home for at least three months now, and still, they couldn't figure out why she'd not been in the system for that amount of time. It was as if when she decided to retire from the Army, they decided that she was no longer employed by them and hadn't gotten paid. She didn't know what she was going to do if it didn't come to her soon. Things were getting rough.

"I'm sorry, but I can't allow you to live like that, miss. I'd lose my job if I were to allow you to sleep in your car. And if anything happened to you, well, I'd be feeling guilty for the rest of my days." He pulled out his cell phone, and she thought for sure he was going to call the police on her. "I'm going to call my missus, and you can sleep in one of our spare bedrooms. It won't be any trouble at all."

"I can't do that. You don't even know me." He told her that he had a good sense of character. "But I'm a complete stranger to you. For all you know, I could be a mass murderer and kill both you and your wife."

"It'll be fine." While he spoke to whom she assumed was his wife, she tried to think where she could go to sleep. There was no way that she was going to go to his house to sleep. That was just about as ridiculous as her not getting her paychecks. Whatever he said to his wife, he was giving her the thumbs up. They both might be nice people, but why would they take in someone off the streets? "Look, officer—I didn't get your name."

"Telly Markus. My parents thought it was a fun name. Get it, Telly Markus, like telemarketer." She didn't get it, but he thought it was funny, so she laughed as well. "It's all set up. If you'll just follow me over to the next street, my wife will be waiting for you in the doorway."

"This is very generous of you, but out of the question." He said they had an extra shower too. He told her how their kids were all moved out now, and they had plenty of room. "But I'm a stranger."

"What's your name?" She told him she was
Elaine Westcock. "See, now we're not strangers
anymore. My wife's name is Brenda Markus. Nothing
funny about her name." She still hadn't caught on to
his name but only nodded at him. "You'll be able to
get a fresh shower in the morning, and won't it be nice
to be able to have a hearty breakfast before you go to
your interview. I know good things are going to come
your way, Ms. Westcock. See that it don't."

"I could use a bit of good luck." She was bullied
into going to his house and staying. There was no
other way around it. If she didn't stay, he was going
to have to arrest her for not having any place to sleep,
and then she'd be late getting to the open interviews
at the school. She didn't think it was right, but she
didn't want to be arrested either, when she needed this
job more than anything that she'd ever done before.
"You'll have to let me pay you for messing up your
evening."

"I didn't have to fill out paperwork, so you
saved me a bit of time. I'm getting off at eleven, and
now I can go home thinking I did something good for a
change. I don't particularly care for making arrests. This
town is quiet all the time in the evening, but sometimes
things happen. You've made my night. I love helping
people." She thought him a generous man if not a little
on the too-trusting side. She could have been anyone.

"You'll be fine as rain. Just go on to see my wife there, and you'll see, things will be better in the morning for you, having a good night's sleep, not in the jail."

She'd been bullied or blackmailed; she didn't know for sure which, but she was going to enjoy having a bed rather than the back seat of her car. Then there was the shower that she was looking forward to, instead of washing up at a rest stop. Yes, she supposed that being bullied into something like this was good.

Mrs. Markus had the bed all made up for her when she arrived. There was also a plate of food for her to eat, as well as clean towels for her to take a shower with. She didn't get this kind of service at home, much less in the rest stops where she'd been sleeping until tonight. Thanking the woman several times for her hospitality, she was in the little bedroom before ten-thirty. Snuggling down in the covers, she decided that if she was going to be homeless after tonight, she was going to look back on this night with fondness and be thankful that there were still kind people in the world.

She didn't stir at all. Elaine did wake up once and fell back to sleep when she heard something in the room. But since she didn't see anything, she went back to sleep and slept until Mrs. Markus woke her at seven the next morning. After taking a refreshing shower and getting dressed in her nicer clothing, she made her way to the kitchen to have herself a nice cup of tea. Apparently, she was having breakfast with the mister, too, as he was just as chipper this morning as he'd been last evening.

In the bright sunlight of the room, she could see that they were an older couple. More than likely in their late fifties to early sixties. She thought Telly, as he'd asked her to call him, was a little old for the police force. But he answered her question before she could think it all the way through. He was set for retirement in a couple of months and was looking forward to it. They were the cutest couple that she'd ever met and told them so.

"Oh, go on with you." She smiled at Brenda and told her that it was true. "Well, I hope you get the job today. They've been looking for teachers since the mess up before." She told her about the scandal from before, and it was terrible to hear how so many teachers had gotten into trouble over it. "Some of those teachers should have been fired if you ask me. Those Erickson men, they're good ones too. Old lady Grable did them well when she passed away. I'm glad that she had them. There is no telling what that son of hers would have done had they not been around to keep him on his p's and q's."

She hadn't heard of Mrs. Grable, but would love to hear the story; but she was being pushed out the door to her interview, and it would have to wait for another day. Driving to the lot that surrounded the school, she thought she could see herself working here every day. Elaine thought that if she didn't get the job, she'd be depressed again. It was difficult being out of work for so long, and she couldn't wait to land herself some kind of job.

There were already two people in front of her when she got to the school. While waiting her turn, there were three more who came in behind her, and she wondered where they came from. No one at the desk seemed to know anyone who was applying, or perhaps that was a ploy. Perhaps they did know them and were pretending not to.

When she was next in line, she pulled out her resume and thought about what she was going to say about being out of work. She'd been out of the service for four months now, and she'd been traveling the states. All true, but she'd been looking for a place to work, too. After being in the service for ten years, she thought it was time she tried something else. That was all true. She looked up when the woman who had gone in front of her came out.

"Ms. Westcock?" She stood up and pulled her things with her. When one of the women sitting next to her put out her foot to no doubt trip her, she stepped over her and into the room. When they were both seated, Mr. Sheen laughed. "I do believe she was going to trip you up and make you look clumsy. She won't get the job even if she has a perfect resume. I don't want pranksters in my school."

He looked over her resume and asked her standard questions. Why she wanted to teach at their school nearly tripped her up, but she decided that she wasn't going to bullshit her way through the interview. She told him they were hiring and she thought she'd be a good fit for the job. At his laughter, she felt embarrassed.

"I'm sorry to laugh, but that's about the most honest answer I've had in the two weeks that we've been interviewing people. I love it." She told him how she'd been home for a few months now and was needing a job. "I know another service woman. She's just retired as well. But she's a doctor. Married to one of the Erickson men."

"I've heard about the scandal. It was top news for a while." He said that they'd never thought it would make the national feed. "I heard about it when I was in Kentucky for an interview. It's all anyone can talk about is how they had padded their wants for their classroom. If I had an opportunity to have something for my room that usually isn't provided, it would be a nice little fridge. I love cold water, and I'm sure some of the students would like one once in a while as well."

"One of the teachers wanted cases of paper

plates and napkins for her hog roast at the end of the year. She didn't think that they'd look at the list all that hard and wouldn't bother with a few extras, so she could use them. Plastic ware as well." She said she couldn't believe some people. "I was shocked. And to think that the Ericksons had donated all the extras that the teachers need is something that I just can't get over."

They talked for about half an hour, and she told him how she'd come to be in Tennessee when she lived in West Virginia. They were getting along nicely when she remembered this wasn't a social call but an interview. He seemed to have been slightly embarrassed by it as well. Once she stood up and gathered her things, he told her that they had to do a background check, but for her to count on having the job if she passed. That was the best news she's had all day, and she told him so.

"Good. I like you and think we can get along nicely as teachers here. Just tell me which grade it is that you wish to teach, and I'll put your name in that slot." She told him kindergarten. She loved the first-year students who came in to learn. "I have your name and file right here. While I usually call them in once a day to have the background checks, I'm going to send yours in right now." She left the office while he was calling it in.

Excitement made her feel good, so when the woman who tried to trip her looked up at her, she stuck her tongue out at her. It was petty and childish, but she didn't care. She'd tried to trip her so that she'd look foolish, and that wasn't right. As soon as she was in her car, she did a little dance with the steering wheel. She had a job. She wasn't the least bit worried about the background check. She'd done nothing wrong in all her life.

Now she just needed to find a place to rent until she got her checks from the service, and she'd be all right. Giddy with the knowledge that she had something to work with, she dipped into her stash and bought herself a much-needed coffee. It was something that she rarely indulged in, but today was something special.

~*~

Knox had just finished up the background checks on his staff when Locke called him to tell him that he had one more for him to do today. As he was getting the information from him, typing it into the program as he went, Locke was telling him how they'd hired a kindergarten teacher if things went well.

"That's wonderful news. I know that the school was having trouble filling that slot. I would think that's the easiest of all the classes to teach. They don't know anything but what she teaches them." Locke said he thought it would be the hardest because kids would be missing their parents and all, and be weepy all day. "I guess I never thought of that. I remember going to kindergarten and having the time of my life. I guess they have to know a whole list of things before they can get into the classroom."

"Preschool is what they recommend now. If kids don't go to preschool, they're behind in their needs. I remember going to preschool, and all we learned how to do was share the toys. I guess they have a lot of stuff they had to learn now." He said that kids were getting smarter all the time. "I believe it. I know that when I'm having computer problems, I call Marcie's son to help me out. I don't have them often, but he also hooked up my wireless printer for me. For a wireless printer, it certainly had a great many wires."

"You sound like an eighty-year-old man." They both laughed. "Just so you know, I'd not tell that story again to anyone if I were you. They'll make fun of you."

"Probably. But it did confuse me when I had to hook it up to the internet, too. I don't mean to sound old here, but I'm feeling it on somedays." Again, he told him not to repeat what he'd said because he was sounding older all the time. "All right. Do you have anything on that person yet? I know that the first research is usually quick."

"It says that she'd not had any arrests, no

outstanding warrants, nor does she have any leans on a house. In fact, she doesn't own one." Locke said that was good to know. "As far as I can see, she's okay to hire. I'll do a deeper background check, but I don't see any problems with her non-service record. I'll do that one now."

"I didn't realize that she'd been in the service. I wonder if she's heard of Shipley? I don't know why she would, it's a lot of people, but wouldn't it be cool if they'd been friends or something?" He said he was sounding old again. "Why, because I want to see if my sister-in-law knows someone? Now you're just grasping at straws just to make fun of me."

"You make it too easy at times." He read off the rest of the report on Elaine Westcock. "It says that she was in the service for ten years and retired in the last few months. She was an elementary teacher before she joined up and has been keeping up with her certification for all that time. She's well qualified for the job, I think."

"I'm glad to hear that. One less teacher that we have to worry about teaching at the school." Knox read on about her stay in the service and was impressed. She'd been a duty nurse too and had worked on the front line. She might well know Shipley or at least know of her. He decided to call her to find out if she'd heard of Westcock. "I'm going to go to the doctor with

Alex. You let me know when you get her military background check done, and I'll let David know. I think he really wants this woman working for him."

After ending the call with his brother, he finished up the paperwork that had been piling up on his desk since the thing with the teachers. He'd been running point on the advertising and wording of things like what they required in a teacher for them. Even filing the contract they'd be required to sign once they were vetted to be teachers. The board approved the contract on the first go, and it made him feel pretty good about himself. He didn't much get to do that sort of thing unless it was with his brother, Zander.

Both he and Zander were attorneys, but Zander did all the courtroom stuff. He'd do the research and write up what he'd found for his brother, so he didn't have to go to the courtroom. It wasn't that he didn't know how to be there when a trial was going on—he usually sat in the courtroom with his brother while he was handling the case. Knox would get too nervous about going to the hearing and was terrified of messing up. They worked well together, and both of them loved what they did for their firm.

After he was able to clear off his desk, he made his way to the kitchen. He would get a snack about this time of day and wasn't surprised when there were veggies and dip for him to eat. It made him sound like he was a kid getting his after-school snack, but he burned a lot of energy when he was working and didn't care who made fun of him because of it.

"I have a list of people that we can hire to replace the two who have quit working here with you." Shirley, his cook, told him she'd make the calls if he wanted her to. "That would be fantastic. I'm taking your advice and hiring three more rather than just the two, so that we have someone to work part-time. I'll let you decide on which person gets the part-time position. They all three said they'd take what I could give them."

"Very good. I'm going to be narrowing it down to one more in the kitchen, too. I need to retire soon, and having someone to just step into the role I'm creating will make it easier on you and your household." He said that he hated to see her go. "Well, now that I've broken my hip and have had it replaced, I want to work at home more. It don't bother me hardly, but by the end of the day, I'm hurting."

"Maybe you'll see something in the person we hire, and you'll stick around for a bit longer. Not that I want you hurting, but we've had a good long time together." She told him that they'd had nine years of being cook for him, and she was going to miss him. "I'm going to miss you as well. I will also miss your biscuits and gravy on Saturday morning. You make the best."

"You just like my biscuits. I'll teach the new cook how you like them. Never would have thought of covering them in bacon grease when I bake them, but they sure are tasty." He was craving her biscuits then, but didn't say anything to her. She'd be whipping him up a batch when he knew that she had already made several loaves of bread for the rest of the week. "You're going to find you a girlfriend someday and forget all about me and my biscuits."

"Never. I might even have you come back to teach her how to make them so that I can have them when the cook has a day off." She laughed with him, and he finished up his light snack. "I'm going to go see my brothers in a little while. Do you need anything from town?"

After telling him she had it all, he made his way out to his car. It was getting chilly out now, and the trees had about lost all their leaves. He loved the crunch of them under his footfalls, and the colors always reminded him that natural colors were the best. Most of his house was in the same colors as fall, and he wouldn't change it out no matter what. It was soothing to him, unlike the other tones that his brothers used in their homes.

Deciding to walk into town, he was nearly there when he noticed that someone was in the realtor's office. They had those big desk-to-ceiling windows in the place, which he never understood, to make sure that they looked busy all the time. Instead of keeping out the sunlight, he thought that the place must have been flooded with light all the time, making it hard to read the computers. That's what he thought about every time he looked over to their building. And the cleaning bill for all those windows must cost a fortune each week.

He found Demi at his restaurant and was glad to see that the *Crockery Pot* was still doing so well now that his brother had retired from it and was working at the school. He cooked breakfast for the kids at the school every morning, and he seemed to be having a good time. Just as he was entering the *Pot*, he noticed that he had his kids with him. He loved his young nephews very much.

"How's it going?" He told him that they were just going out for ice cream. "Mind if I join you? I have a couple of questions for your dad." Martin said it was fine with him, and Teddy asked him if he'd done anything today that would allow him to have a treat. "I have. Today I cleaned off my desk and got things filed away in the correct drawers. I feel really good about that."

"Then you deserve a treat. Martin and I helped Dad by sorting out the potatoes that he got in. Some of them are bakers, and the others are going to be used for mashed. I love mashed potatoes." He said they were his favorite, too, with lots of gravy. "No, not gravy but butter. I love me some melted butter on my mashed."

He loved it when the boys called Demi dad. He wasn't really their father, but you'd never know it to talk to them. Mandy, Demi's wife and aunt to the two boys, had come as a package deal when he met her, and he'd fallen in love with the three of them. Every one of them loved the little family and loved to see Demi and Mandy handling them. He'd bet at times they could be a handful, too.

They made their way to the ice cream shop on foot. During the day, it wasn't so cold out if you had on a jacket, but at night, when the sun went down, it was freezing cold. Not really that cold, he thought, but cold enough to make you wish you were home and in bed instead of out in it. The ice cream shop was busy when they got there.

"They'll be closing soon. Not much sales in the winter for ice cream." He said he thought they'd be open year-round because they served hamburgers and other sandwiches, too. "Not to hear them talk about it. I love ice cream year-round, but I guess they don't make enough sales to warrant having salespeople around and the lights on. They're having a sale for the next couple of days to get rid of all the stuff that they didn't sell this summer. I heard that Friday was their last day open."

"Well, that sucks. I like coming here for a quick lunch." The new owners had only owned the place for a year now and were doing a good job so far. But he wondered if they were closed up for winter, how many sales they'd miss when people got used to buying ice cream for their homes. It was much cheaper that way. Not as fun, but for sure much cheaper. "I guess I'll have to preorder from your place when I'm working late and need dinner when Shirley is off."

He told his brother that his cook was retiring soon because her hip was bothering her too much to continue working for him. Knox said how much he was going to miss her meals, and Demi agreed with him. He'd forgotten how many times his brother would show up for breakfast on his way to work in the morning. Since getting married, he'd not been by once. Also, he blamed it on cooking for school as well.

As they finished up their cones, they walked around the town. Knox had been running on sidewalks since he'd moved here and did it every day. Some of his brothers would join him sometimes when he was out, but not so often now that they were all married, but for him and Zander. He missed them doing things with him, but he was glad for their Thursday night meals they had as a group. Knox didn't know what he'd do if they still didn't do that.

"Have you had any word on the teachers? I was wondering how the open interviews were going." He told him what he knew about the kindergarten teacher, but that was about all he knew. "Are they coming in and not passing the background check or what?"

"That's it. Because we do such a deep background check, a lot of them aren't passing the grade. I'm glad that we do such a deep one; otherwise, we might get someone in there that we don't want and can't get rid of." He said he'd not thought of that. "Of the four we need to hire, I think that only two have passed the checks. Most of them have some kind of record in their background that prevents them from teaching at the school. I don't know about you, but I'm happy for the deeper checks. It'll keep the kids safe who go there."

"I agree. My kids go there, and I'm thrilled about it." They talked about the upcoming holidays and what was going to be done. Locke and Amy had gone all out in what they were doing around their home, and not to be outdone, the rest of them were trying to beat them. Last he looked, Locke had more blow-ups than were on display at the local stores that sold them. He wondered where he was getting them from.

He never got around to asking his brother his questions, but that was all right. He'd get him next time he saw him. They weren't that important anyway. He needed to talk to Locke more, but since he was out of town this morning, he'd have to wait on him, too. Oh well, he'd gotten out of the house some today, and that was always good.

Chapter 3

Elaine knew that her background check would come back clean. She'd never even had a ticket in her life, much less anything else that might ding her. So she didn't have any problem signing a one-year lease with the realtor on a two-bedroom place that even had a washer and dryer set up. Not that she could afford herself a set, but someday she might. All she had in the way of furniture was an air mattress and a laundry basket for her clothing. So long as she was set with those, the rest could come later, she told herself.

She had fifty-two dollars left to her name until she got paid. That was after she'd gotten a full tank of gas to drive back and forth to school. Even if something happened and she didn't get the job, she did notice that the pizza place was hiring, and she could do that for a while. She just needed her checks to come in from the army so she could afford groceries, too.

Making the call again, she was surprised when someone knocked on her car door and found that it was a woman whom she didn't know. Asking her to wait a moment, she finished up her confusing call and finally hung up. They were still looking for the reason that she hadn't been paid, but they had the checks now. Telling them that she needed them only had her more frustrated. They needed to find out the reason for the mess-up, and that was why they were holding off on sending them out.

Getting out of her car, she smiled at the woman. She didn't know her, but figured that she just wanted her to move her car or something. Not that she was parked illegally or anything, but some people were like that. She asked her what she could do for her.

"My name is Shipley. Well, it's really Candace Shipley, but I go by my last name." She'd heard the name before but didn't know the person or even if this was her. "I think we might well have worked together out of the country."

"On the front line." She nodded and grinned. "I never actually worked with you, but I've heard of you. It's a small world. How did you know where to find me? It's not like I've advertised that I have an address yet."

"My brother-in-law did a background check on you, and it hit the Washington office where I was stationed from. I do a little work for them now and again, but nothing like going to the front line to operate. How's it going? I couldn't help but overhear that you were having trouble getting your last checks. The same thing happened to me." She said that it's been four months now, and she still hasn't gotten her checks. "They're giving you the run around, I'm betting too."

"That's right. And I could really use the money." She wondered why she was able to talk to her about this and realized that she'd somehow gotten her to the little Dari Twist that was across the street, where she'd been parked. "I've eaten already, but you go ahead."

"You've not eaten, and it's my treat." She felt a little of her temper get the better of her, so she let out long breaths until she had some control over it. "Feel better? I'm going to get some information from you, and we'll see about making a couple of calls to get your checks to you today. I have just enough pull to get it done."

"If you can do that, I'll look over the fact that you bullied me into coming here." The menu was sort of sparse, but she was able to get a hamburger with some fries. Shipley got the same, but instead of a bottle of water, she got herself a milkshake. They finished it off while talking about her leaving the service. "I've been out for four months, and I was able to get that last check before leaving, then nothing. They said it was a computer glitch, but I don't know. It's taking forever. Now they tell me that they've got my checks, but can't send them out until they figure out what has happened. Like I said, I could really use the money."

"No kidding. Let me make a call." While she

was on her cell phone, she looked around the little area. There were a lot of teenagers hanging around the place, and she wondered if this was the spot to be in the summer months. Then she realized that they were selling ice cream at a discount and figured that was why they were here. She didn't listen in on the call that Shipley was making, even though it was about her, but did keep an ear on it so that when she finished talking, she could get the information that hopefully she could use. "Do you have an address?" She rattled off the new one that she'd gotten just this morning.

"I've also got a post office box, but they said they'd not mail them to that." She nodded and continued with her call. Elaine decided that since this was on her way home, she might make use of their lunch menu in the summer months to save on cooking. She hated to cook more than she hated being without money. When Shipley got off the phone, she was grinning. "You got them mailed to me."

"Yes, you'll get them in the morning. I made a call to the vice president. He's married to one of the other women's sister. They've been married about a month now, and it's wonderful having that contact." She said that was impressive. "It is, isn't it? I'm so glad that I could help you. My husband's name is Dusty Erickson."

"Now that's a name I've heard a great deal

about since being here. They're the ones that caught the teachers padding their want list when they asked for things to get them through the end of the year, right?" She said that was right and was happy to be related to them. "They must have a great deal of pull when it comes to the schools around here. That's all the people around here can talk about is the great Erickson brothers and their wives."

"They're a good bunch of men. They've lived here for the last twelve or thirteen years now and have done wonders for not just the school but the town as well. It's been great living in this little town, too. I hope you like it." She said that she was sure that she would now that she had her money and a job. "I heard that you're teaching one of the classes at the school. Congratulations on that. We've needed new teachers for over a month now, and I'm glad to know that you're one of them."

"I'd been in the service since I got out of college. I taught for a while, but then realized that I couldn't make the kind of money that I would if I continued my education in the service. So I enlisted and got an education that was good, and learned a few things while I was in there. I'm just hoping that they don't find anything in my background check that keeps me from working." She said that she had it on good authority that she'd passed. "Good to know. I just signed a one-year lease with an apartment, and even with my money coming to me, I might have a hard time making my rent each month."

"You'll be fine. I know it." As they finished their meals, they talked about the little town. She told her how she'd spent the night at an officer's home last night, and she knew who it had been. "The Markuses have been around for a long time. They're allowing Telly to work out his retirement even though he's having trouble with his nerves. He's the calmest man I've ever met, until something goes wrong, then he's really bad. He gets the shakes and stammers, too. But he's calm most of the time."

They talked about the other teachers who weren't coming back. Only four so far, but she had a feeling that they weren't going to show up on Monday morning at all and quit without notice. She could see a bunch of people doing that too. Just to make the school short-staffed.

"They didn't take too kindly to being laid off without pay. It was only for a month, but that could have been the difference between them having money for a mortgage payment or not. But they're the ones that had done it, so they have no one to blame but themselves." Elaine agreed with her and said that she could never do that. "I didn't think you would. I actually didn't think that a couple of the teachers would, but peer pressure can be a lot even when you're an adult."

By the time the sun was going down and the weather was getting colder, they parted ways. But not before a dinner invitation was given to her by Shipley. She said that she usually got together with her sisters-in-laws once a week and thought that she could use a couple of friends since she was new to the area. She didn't know how much she'd have in common with the Erickson women, but she thought that she could use a couple of friends. So she agreed to have dinner with them on Thursday night.

On her way to her car, she noticed that the kids had all gone and the place was closing up. She'd heard that they would be closing for the winter months on Friday and was going to miss just being able to get a lunch or two there.

Driving home, she got to her place in less time than she remembered it took. Getting out of her car, she tried to judge the distance between her place and the school and realized that she could just walk to school when the weather permitted. She loved that idea and was going to do it when she started. There was no point in taking her car there if walking was just as easy.

Setting her alarm for seven since her check was supposed to be here from eight to night, she was excited to be able to know that the money was coming in. Looking on her laptop for the first time in several weeks, she was also excited to be able to have internet in her new place. Cable was also included, but since she didn't have a television set, she was just going to be watching whatever she could on her computer for a while.

She did some online shopping while she was getting ready for bed. The first thing she was going to need was a bed so that she could get a good night's sleep. The one night that she'd had at the Markus place had made her realize that she couldn't sleep on the floor for very long. It was hard on her back and legs. Not to mention towels and other linens that would do her a world of good in her apartment.

There was a towel packed up in her things. She would sometimes use the truck stop's showers when she needed to get a good washing. They had laundry mats as well, which she used and had done quite well for herself. The only thing that she didn't have was cookware, and she'd been doing well without that. It wasn't as if she was going to be cooking herself a five-course meal anytime soon. Just a plate and a few pieces of silverware, and she'd do fine. She put that on her list of things to get when she got her checks.

She was nearly too excited to go to bed that night. The sleeping bag was nice to rest on, but to sleep a good night's sleep was something else. She'd have to get her a bed with a good mattress soon, or she'd be too uncomfortable to teach the children with her back aching all the time. That was going to be a priority for her to get, no matter what else was on her list.

Waking before the alarm went off, she took a shower and enjoyed the freedom of it being all hers. Once she had dried her hair and pulled it back in a ponytail, she got out the required paperwork for her to claim her checks. They said that they'd write her three of them because the taxes would have been horrific. That way, too, she could cash them easier than one lump sum. Giddy with the thought of having money again, she waited by the door, sitting on the floor until the doorbell rang. At eight o'clock right on the nose, the doorbell rang, and it was an army courier who had an envelope for her. As soon as she was able to verify that it was her, the man was on his way, and she was standing in the kitchen reading the note from the vice-president of the United States.

"My dear Elaine, I'm so sorry for the confusion about your money. It shouldn't have been a problem for you, and I'm glad I was able to make it work out for you. There is a little extra in the form of a fourth check so that you can know that we here at the White House take getting paid for our servicemen and women very seriously. I'm again sorry that it took so long, and I was glad that Shipley was able to get through to me to get it done. I feel like a hero." He signed it

with his first name.

There was also a postscript that gave her his personal phone number in the event that he could do anything more for her. The fourth check was for the same amount as she'd had in the other three checks, and she was beyond happy about it.

While she was finishing up with her list, she got a call from Mr. Sheen about the job. She'd gotten the job as a kindergarten teacher and would start the following Monday morning. Dancing around her new place, she thought perhaps things were finally going her way.

~*~

Knox didn't know what to make of Shipley telling him about the woman that she'd just met. He didn't know if she was setting him up or just being polite. They'd been pushing him into having a wife for the past several weeks now, and he was getting aggravated about it. Not that he'd say he was pissed off to Shipley, but he'd grumble under his breath about it. He wasn't that stupid as to tell her she was butting in where it was none of her business. But he did find that he wanted to meet the young woman who had gotten such rave comments from the division that she was a part of in the service.

"I was wondering if you had about an hour that I could bounce things off with you?" He told his brother Zander that he was forever there for him. "I figured you'd say that. I have this case coming up with Carrie, and I was wondering if you could tell me if I'm pushing too hard in wanting to have Carrie there when the trial starts. She doesn't want to go, but I think that it would go a long way with the judge if she were to show him how much they'd hurt her when they wanted the checks."

"I'd say that you'd have to talk to her about it. I'd tell her what you just told me and see what she has to say about it." He said he had, and she refused to go. "Then you have your answer. She's not going to be bullied into anything that she doesn't want to do. I understand that she should be there, if nothing else than to show support to you about the trial. But she's been terrorized enough with them. Not to mention how many times they've beaten her up over the money. If she doesn't want to go, then there isn't anything you can say to make her go."

"I figured you'd say that. Even Shipley said the same thing about bullying her into going. I can understand it, but they'll be under guard with the police, not to mention I've requested that they be chained up as well. I don't want to take any chances either." He asked if she'd told her that part. "I only just requested it and was granted the way things would go today. I never thought of that making a difference."

"It would to me." He nodded and said that he'd have to tell her what he'd done. "Also, if I were you, I'd request more armed guards and police around the courthouse as well. Like you said, you don't want to take any chances with them getting loose. And if they do, you know that they'll kill Carrie, if for no other reason than they will blame her for being in jail. They won't make it easy on her, either, given the chance to get at her. I'd tell her that part, and then if she still disagrees about going, then let it go. She has her own nightmares about them that we'll never understand. Even though our father beat us, they were her siblings, and that has to hurt worse. Especially since she was helping with their mother."

"All right. I don't have to like it, but I'm going to do what you said, also, about the extra police around. I think it would maybe make them think twice—never mind. They'll never think twice about anything if they can get away with it. Even when there isn't any way for them to get by, they'll do what they want and damn the consequences." Knox agreed with his brother. "Did you know that the police are having a hard time with the group of them? They're demanding that they have special treatment for no other reason than they want it. I'd have shot the lot of them if I had been in charge of them."

"I suppose it's a good thing we're not in charge,

I guess." They both laughed and decided that if they were in charge of the family, they would have put them in prison without a trial and been done with them. See how long they lasted in the kind of environment, such as a prison. "Not long, I'm betting. They'd bully the wrong person, and that would be the end of them all."

After making a couple of phone calls, not only did Zander have the extra hands on duty that might be needed, but there was also going to be police on the outside of the courthouse in the event that they tried to escape. He didn't know how that was going to happen with them chained up, but he would not doubt anything coming from the group of them for any amount of money. They were terrible people, and the sooner they were in prison, the better off the little town would be. He'd even found other families that had been knocked around by them that were willing to testify against them, so long as they weren't getting out to hurt them. People were terrified of them and with good reason. They were a group of people that you'd find one or two of in a family, but it was all of them, save Carrie.

He was headed home after talking with his brother when he saw a woman trying to get her furniture into an apartment. He'd heard that the place had been rented, as he owned the place, but he hadn't any idea that she was already moving in. He made his way across the street to see if he could help her get things inside, as it was starting to rain.

"Thank you, that would be wonderful." He didn't have any trouble getting the mattress in, as she'd already gotten the bed in by herself. There were boxes everywhere. "I didn't have to pay extra for things to be delivered, but now that I've been working at this for the last hour, I wish I had."

"We'll get it. Let me help you get the bed set up. Do you have any tools?" She didn't, and looked like she was ready to cry. "It's been a long day, I'm betting, so let me go to my house and pick up my toolbox. I'll be back soon."

He knew who she was but didn't bother with introductions. As soon as he was at his house, he picked up his toolbox and ordered dinner for the two of them too to be delivered. He had a feeling that she hadn't eaten all day, which was why she looked so defeated. He would be too if he had to move into his place again without the help of his brothers. Just as he was pulling into the parking lot, it started to rain like the heavens had opened up. He rushed into the apartment and was already soaked.

"I don't even know who you are, and here I am allowing you to help me put together my bed. I must really be tired to have done that. I'm usually very cautious." He told her how he'd ordered food for the two of them and told her his name. "Knox Erickson. I'm betting you're one of the Ericksons that pretty much run things around here." She looked at him oddly. "I'm sorry. That was uncalled for. I'm just really stressed out and hungry. You were right in thinking that I hadn't eaten all day."

They got the bed put together in no time at all, and the rental truck was locked up for the night by the time they got all the boxes of things that she'd gotten as well. She'd gotten a lot of things locally for which he was proud of her for and the few things that she'd had to get out of town were things that he knew wouldn't have been something that the local shops would have sold. The mattress and box springs being one of them.

It took them until ten to get things put away. After eating their subs, they stood around talking about the new job she had, and he was glad that he'd been able to make sure that her background checks had been done in a timely manner. Once he was finished with the last of the boxes, he took them out to the dumpster and tossed them inside. He felt good about helping Elaine and was happy that she trusted him enough to allow him to help.

"I'm afraid it would have taken me days to get things finished without your help. If you'd allow me to pay you something for your help, I'd be appreciative. It was a lot of work that, like I said, would have taken me forever to get finished and cleaned up." He told her that it had been his pleasure. "I'm sure that it wasn't. Who wants to spend a Tuesday night unpacking boxes and putting things together? But I do thank you so much."

"It really was my pleasure. I've not done anything like this since I moved into my own home, and it brought back a lot of memories. Good ones. I love to open a box and not know what's in it until then. Yours were a little less guessing as they had right on the box what was in them." She said that she'd started out fresh today. "Good for you. It must be nice to wipe the slate clean and start over. Sometimes I think that I'd like to do that, but I have too many memories in the things that I have."

"I've been overseas for some time now and didn't have a lot to begin with. So this was easy. I made myself a list and stuck to it so that I'd not get too many things that I didn't need." He said that he understood that. "I bet you would. I've heard from the townspeople that you only came here with the shirts on your backs when you broke down in front of what was then called the Grable Mansion. It's a beautiful home."

"My brother and his wife live there now. It's called the Erickson Mansion." He told her how Martha Grable had left it to Locke for taking such good care of her when she'd been alive. "He became a nurse so that when she needed him, he was right there for her. Now he's a doctor and doing very well for himself. Alex is a hoot, and we all love her to pieces."

By eleven, he was headed home. He'd not meant to stay that long, but the company was good, and they'd gotten a great deal of work finished. Getting him something to tide him over, he opened the lid on the stew and shut the refrigerator before sampling some of it before going to bed. He got himself a bowl of cereal before going to bed, and that was all he'd allow himself. He couldn't wait until tomorrow night to have some of the best stew in all the counties.

Knox felt good when he got into bed, like he'd used a few muscles that he hadn't in a while, but didn't strain himself too much where he'd be sore in the morning. It was a good kind of work that made him feel good about himself. And he liked Elaine, too. She was fun to be around.

The next morning, when he got up, he felt a little tender in his shoulders, but was all right after a little bit of walking around and stretching. As soon as he got into his office, he wanted to call Elaine and see if she was sore too, and decided that they didn't know each other that well for him to be checking on how she slept. He found himself thinking about her all morning and into the afternoon, so much so that he finally broke down and called her.

"I was just calling to see if you're all right today. I'm just a little sore." She laughed and told him that she was sore but not too bad right now. "I think that I'd help you again, but try to be in better shape when I do."

"Same here. But it was nice to be able to get up this morning and not have a mess to deal with, so I can't thank you enough for your help. The cup of tea helped too, as I usually have one in the morning before I get going for the day." He said that he did as well; it gave him a little boost when he needed it. "I have to get my books ready for the school year as I'm going to start on Monday. Mr. Sheen said that I could run by at any time and look around the classroom. They've been having a sub teach the class for the last month, and he wants to make sure that I have everything I need."

"I'm going to be heading into town later today. If you need anything, I can pick it up for you. And by town, I mean the next town over. It's one of the larger cities before you get to the major ones." He told her the name of the city he was headed to. "I don't mind picking up anything that you might have forgotten too."

"I think I'm all right. I do have some things that I need to pick up for the classroom, but I want to check with the school first to see what is there. Thank you, however." He told her that she had his number if she thought of something. "I do, and I appreciate you calling me. It's nice to have a friend in town. I'm supposed to meet up with your sisters-in-laws for dinner tomorrow night. I'm both looking forward to that and not. There will be so many of them that I don't know, so I'm a little nervous about meeting them for dinner."

"You'll like them. They're a little pushy but very good to have in your corner. And I guess you've met Shipley." She said that she had and was happy that she had. "Good. I'll talk to you later. Don't forget, you owe me dinner for helping you out."

"I won't forget. I'm looking forward to that as well." When he hung up, he wanted to call her back just so he'd have someone to talk to. Shaking his head, he decided that he'd better get to work on his paperwork or he'd be behind again. He hated to be behind when it came to his job.

Chapter 4

Carrie kept telling herself she'd be all right with her brothers and sisters in the same room, but she didn't believe herself. They were horrific to her, and everyone knew it. She just wanted today over with so that she could go back to somewhat of a normal life and have some fun for a change. Even going to visit her mom when she wanted to would be something she'd not been able to do because of her family. But she did have a good visit yesterday with her mom.

She not only knew who she was, but she was telling her what she'd had for lunch before she'd gotten there as well. After fixing her hair and making sure that her room was tidy, they sat in the front lounge and talked for about an hour before she began slipping away again. It was the saddest part of her visit when her mom no longer knew who she was, nor was she as nice. Mom could and would get combative if she didn't know who you were, and you tried to get her to understand. Carrie usually left in tears after that, and it would hurt her to her soul to have to leave her when she kept wanting to know when she was going to get to go home.

The courtroom was packed, and she didn't understand that. Of course, it took her nearly an hour of waiting for her family's turn to be spoken to in order to understand that they would have their pretrial one at a time. They had opted to be seen that way, so that's the way that the court hearing would go when they got around to that as well. The room was silent when they were brought into the room in cuffs and chains. Christ, they didn't look the same as she remembered them.

"Remember, they can't get to you." She was ever so grateful to Zander for reminding her of that. They really couldn't hurt her the way they were chained up, but that didn't do much for her fear factor. They'd been beating her nearly all her life, and she didn't think there was much out there that would stop them when they wanted to knock her around again. When Allen stood up as well as he could, she grabbed Zander's hand and held onto him. He'd been a good friend to her since this all started, and she knew that he'd keep her safe.

"I wanna know why I'm here." The judge told him he'd get to that when it was his turn. "No. I want to know now. I've been cooped up in that jail for three days now and ain't nobody telling me shit." He was told to watch his language. "I'll do what I want and say it too. Do you know who I am?"

"Allen James Sharp. I know who all of you are. Now sit down and shut up until it's your turn to have a say. Not that I care what you have to say about the matters that brought you here, you're going to have a trial when I say so, and that's final." Allen told him he was the head of the family and that his word was better than the judge's. "Better than mine, you say? Well, if that ain't the funniest thing I've ever heard. Sit down before I have the officers sit you down. Now you'll wait your turn like everybody else has to, and that's the final word I have on the matter."

Allen sat down when two officers came to stand behind him. He didn't look happy, and she was afraid of him again. There was never a time when she wasn't afraid of him, but when he had that look in his eyes, it meant that he was going to be killing someone or close to it soon. He was a mean mother fucker and didn't care who he had to kill to get what he wanted, just like most of her family.

Allen and the others had been treating her like a punching bag since she was a toddler. They'd knock her around and then take whatever she had that had meant something to her, like her dolls that she'd gotten for her birthday. They'd destroy them, then blame it on her when she went to tell on them. She soon learned that her mother wasn't going to stand up to them, any of her children, because she'd been beaten by them as well. Their father had left them all long ago, when she'd been about five and had never returned. She put the blame for the way their mother was on their heads for the way they treated her all these years. The poor woman didn't stand a chance against the bullies that were her children.

Thanks to the Ericksons, she had a good job, and her mother was in a facility that took great care of her. She wasn't beaten anymore, and she had three meals a day too. When she'd been taking care of her mom, it had been hit and miss if there would be enough money for her meds, much less food, when they took her social security check every month. Carrie worked three jobs just to make sure that there was electricity in the house, and they'd take that money too.

When it was Allen's turn finally to talk, all he wanted to know was when he was going to get out of jail so that he could get some money. The judge told him that there wasn't going to be any money unless he was working, and Allen shook his head.

"I have recourses." He asked if he meant resources. Allen hated to be corrected, and this time was no different. "I have ways of getting me some money, and I aim to get it. Carrie is going to start carrying her weight, or she's going to be dead."

"Did you just threaten your sister, Mr. Sharp?" He said that she'd better come through with it or he was going to make sure that their mother was no longer around. "My god, you've just threatened two people in my courtroom, and we've barely gotten started. I'll have you know that you'll not be harming anyone while in here."

"I'm not going to be here forever, now am I? When you get up off your ass and let me go, then I'll be able to knock them around a bit to get what I want. And I always get what I want. Even if I have to knock a few heads together to get it." He looked at the rest of the family with him until he spotted her. Every muscle in her body tensed up when he glared at her. "There you are. What did you do with our mother? If you put her in a nursing home, you can just get her out again. I want her check monthly, and you won't be giving it to anyone else that comes around. They'll know better than to fuck with me."

When he finally looked away toward the judge who was banging his gavel against his desk, all her breath let out at once, and she was dizzy from it. He'd threatened her again, and there wasn't anything that anyone could do about it. She knew that if he got out, she'd be dead because there wasn't any way that she was going to give up her mother to him. She liked her just where she was staying.

Zander stood up so that Allen could no longer see her and told the judge that he had a list of crimes that the family as a whole had committed. He also had a list of things that they did individually that were in a separate file, he told him. As he gave dates and the crimes, she could see that there were a great deal more than them just hurting her. It seemed like everyone in town had had some kind of interaction with her family, and none of it was good.

When he got to the checks that had been stolen and forged, the judge sat up and listened. Carrie was sure that he'd heard it all before and was just listening to him go on about all the seemingly petty stuff that her family had done compared to the checks. The judge had questions as to when the checks had been stolen and by whom. He also wanted to know what was done to them by the police department.

"I can only find where they were arrested the one time for forging the checks. The bank manager had called to say that he knew for a fact that the check he had wasn't signed by Mrs. Sharp and wanted someone to come and arrest Allen. He never made it to jail, it seems, and that was the last time that the bank manager had ever called the police. He didn't cash the checks every time they were brought in, but he did on occasion." The judge wanted to know why he'd cashed them at all. "I don't know, Your Honor. I could never get an answer from him other than it was Allen Sharp that wanted them cashed, and he knew better than to not comply."

"So you're thinking that he threatened the bank,

too, are you?" Zander told the man that he didn't know what to think, as no one was talking to him about it. "And I know you and your brother well enough that you would have left no stone unturned trying to find the answer to that, too. Let me look this over."

As the judge looked over the files that Zander had given him, she looked at her family. Syble was dressed in one of the orange outfits that the jail gave a person, but the others were dressed in their street clothing. Allen had on a suit, which he usually wore when he was walking around town, but the others were in jeans and t-shirts. They weren't clean, any of them, but they looked like they'd spent the last several weeks in a jail cell. If they could stay there for the rest of her life, that would make her feel much better. She knew that she'd live longer.

When the judge cleared his throat, she looked back at him, but not before Allen got her attention. He was making a slit across his throat with his fingers, and she knew what he meant. Yes, she hoped that they stayed in the system for the rest of her long life, or she'd not be around to see that her mom was well taken care of. There was no doubt that Allen would kill her or any of the others. They were all just as bad about hurting her, but Allen was the worst.

"Ms. Carrie Sharp?" She stood up when the judge said her name. "Do you have anything to say about this group before I pass judgment on them?"

"Yes, sir, I do. If you could give me twenty-four hours before they're released so I could get myself out of town and hidden away, I'd appreciate it. And if you can't do that, could you please allow me enough time to get my life in order so that my mom is taken care of with my insurance policy? I don't have much, but it'll be enough to make sure she's not out where they can get to her anytime soon. And her checks will be safe with the nursing home." He said that he had that part under control. "Good then. I don't have anything to say to any of them, however."

"You're going to be dead no matter how much time he gives you to hide out, little sister." Allen only called her that when she'd really pissed him off. "Do you hear me? I'm going to come after you for all this shit that you've laid at my door."

She just stared at the judge, and when he stood up, Allen was taken out of the room, screaming about how he was going to kill her and he'd not make it easy on her either. She was going to be dead, and he, for one, would be happy when she was. Allen's last words about killing her were still echoing around the room when the judge sat back down.

"I have enough evidence here that I'm going to set up a trial date." As he continued on with what he was saying, all her mind could do was center on the fact that her own brother was going to kill her, and there was nothing she could do about it. When Zander grabbed her hand, she laid her head down on the table they were at, and she closed her eyes. She was going to die, and there wasn't shit she could do about it. They'd make it long and drawn out, too. No bullet to the head for her. They'd make her beg for death when they started on her.

She didn't know how long she lay there, but Zander was pulling her out of the seat for the next attorney to sit down. Carrie knew that something had happened, but she didn't know what and would ask Zander when they got outside. In the sunshine, she felt better but no less determined to get her affairs in order so that she could leave as soon as possible. For her to live, she was going to have to leave now in order to get a jumpstart on her family to keep them from finding her. She said as much to Zander when he came up to hug her.

"You didn't hear, I take it. They're going to have a trial in two years — late October two years from now. The judge thinks it will take that long to get the evidence that we already have together. Then the public defender for them asked for an extension, and he was granted it for another year." She asked if they would be in jail all that time. "No, he's sending them off to prison so that there's no overcrowding of the jails here. Isn't that great?"

"They'll be gone for three years in a bigger jail?" He told her that it would be prison and they'd be under lock and key until the time of the trial. "That's wonderful news. Oh my gosh, I never expected it to be that long. Are you still going to be taking the trial?"

"Yes. Knox and I will be the ones who represent you. You've been given a gift of three years, and in all that time, we're going to be digging into everything in their past to make sure that they stay for a good deal longer. Maybe by the time they get out, they'll be too old to try to kill you off. That's what I'm hoping for anyway." She hugged him. "Thank you so much. I can't believe that we got three years of them being in prison. And they'll be taken tonight so that they are no longer a burden on the jail system here. No more visits from you either."

She was thrilled with the news and wanted to dance around with Zander. But he already more than likely thought of her as a nut case. She'd cry at the littlest things lately. As she was headed back to her home, she did dance around a little. They were going away, and she couldn't believe it. She had her freedom back, and she couldn't wait to live like they were no longer in her life.

~*~

Knox read over the lease paperwork for the new

building that was going in towards downtown. The building had been renovated just over the last few months, and now that it was ready to be rented, he had five applicants who wanted to take over the building. It was for residential or business, so he had both kinds of requests for it in his file. He looked at his brother when he came into the room with him. He asked August if he'd go over the rental agreements while he had a background check done on the five people who wanted to rent it.

"Are you charging the same for the rent if it's residential or business? It seems to me that there should be a difference." He said when he put it out there that it was for rent, but he never said what the rent would be. "So you could charge what you want to them and see if they still want it. What's the building like? I mean, is it one that could be viable for a family of, say, four people?"

"I think it's too small for a family of four. It has two bedrooms in it now, but there's no room for a third or fourth bedroom. All it has are the two bedrooms, one bath, and a living room, and a kitchen area. It's all on one floor, too." He said that the applicant for the house rental was five people. "Then they probably don't want it. It'll be extremely too small for them. I wonder why they put in an application?"

"There isn't much in the way of rentals around

here. Perhaps they're desperate to find something to live in." Knox said that he'd have to tell them it's not large enough for a family of five. He wasn't even sure it was big enough for a business. "One of the business rentals said they want to turn it into a sub shop. What was it before? I seem to think it was something along those lines, and they couldn't make it work."

"You're right, and it took us a while to get them to get their stuff out, too. Had we known that, we could have just let them sell it to the new renters." August asked about the smell. "It was everywhere, but as soon as we painted it, the smell was better. Like much better than it was before."

"Good to know. The last two places that want to rent it want to change it into a retail store. Again, I don't know how that's going to work with it being so small, not to mention so far off from the downtown area. No one will walk that far to get to their shop." He said that he had thought of that and put it in the advertising when he'd written the place up. "If I were you, I'd just make it a rental for a household. That way, someone with a couple of kids would be all right for a while. A business would just fail again, and that would be another person that we'd have to get out when they do."

"All right. I think that you're right. I'm going to make sure that the people who want to rent understand that it's too small for a family of their size and wouldn't work." August said that he'd help him if he needed it. "I thank you, but I think I got it all right. Have you looked over the rentals for the strip mall that's nearly finished? I hate calling it that, but I don't know what else to call it. It's a strip of stores that has five different buildings in it. One of them is already rented. The other four have had a couple of lookers but nothing more. If you're getting people interested, you'll have to let me know so that I can do the background checks on them."

"Like you said, there is only one that is rented, and as for the others, I have had a few inquiries, but nothing yet. It's off the main street, so I don't think anyone will want to move out that far to try and have a shop. Unless it's really good food, then maybe." He said that it had been sitting empty since before Martha had passed away. "Yes, she left it to me to see if I could get it going. The only thing that I can see moving out that far is a tire shop or something like that. No ladies' shops. I've noticed that they don't do well unless there is a good food place to go as well." He laughed at his brother about not having ladies' shops. "What? You know what I mean? Stops that cater to women that sort of thing."

"Don't let the others hear you say that. Your wife will kill you." He said that he had facts to support his saying that. "Doesn't matter if NASA said it, she wouldn't take too kindly to you telling her that a ladies' shop needs a food place, or it wouldn't do well." They both laughed at that, but he did notice that August looked around to see if his wife was close. They were all afraid of their spouses.

Knox called the family and told them that he thought that the rental was much too small for them. They still wanted to see it, and he was all right with that. But he was going to draw the line at them moving in. It wouldn't do well for anyone to be crowded into a house that small. He set up a time and day for them to go and look at it. August called the businesses and said that even though it was marked as a business, the place was too small for anything of value to go into the place. They, like the couple, wanted to see if they could make it work, and he was all for it. It would be another failed business, and he didn't want to have to clean up after them when they left.

"What do you know about the new teacher in town?" Knox immediately thought of Elaine and almost told his brother that she was off limits to anyone single. "She's a looker, I hear, and is filling out the spot nicely at the school."

"There are three teachers that you could be talking about. All three of them are doing a good job so far, as I've heard. And like we figured when we started helping the school board in getting new teachers, three more quit that just didn't show up on Monday morning." He told him she was the kindergarten teacher. "Elaine Westcock. She's doing really well. Are you thinking about talking to her about Zander?"

"I was wondering if either one of you had dated her yet, yes. I didn't mean to step on your toes if you're already seeing her." Knox said that other than helping her move in, he wasn't seeing her socially. Not yet, anyway. "All right. I'll leave it alone then. Zander doesn't seem to be willing to date much either. Have the two of you formed a pact of some sort that you're not dating anyone?"

"No, nothing like that. But we have been busy with Carrie's case. It's been a long time in coming around. But I'm glad to see that it's paid off finally." He said that he was as well. When he'd spoken to Carrie, she seemed to have a weight lifted off her shoulders. "I would imagine that she has. I can't imagine walking around waiting for one of you guys to knock the shit out of me at any time. They've done enough damage to her, I would say."

They talked about how much work Carrie and Mandy were doing for the older generation in town. They'd had several classes now in teaching women and men how to use a computer to order online and to run a household with a computer in mind. Ordering groceries was the biggest class that they held, and so far, everyone who went through the classes had good things to say about it. He was very proud of them for doing it with the Martha Grable Foundation.

"Did you hear that this week's dinner is going to be at Locke's house? He said that there's a pregame on television for Thursday night and he wants to watch it with us." He said that he'd not heard, but that sounded fantastic. "Yeah, I guess he's ordering food in so that we can have a variety. I'm just hoping that he has the kind of food he did last year for the end of season games. That was a blast."

"He does know how to get food done up well." Knox laughed and told him about the mess-up last month when he'd ordered food for a meeting. "It was all fresh food, and the people looked at it like it was garbage. No one ate any of it because it was things like fresh vegetables and fruit. I wish I could have seen his face when he had it all set up for them. It must have been a disaster."

"Yeah, but I heard that he did the same thing the next month with a meeting. Those people enjoyed it a great deal. I guess it depends on the people that he's meeting with." Knox agreed and said that he loved a fresh layout. "I do as well. It's not something that I want to eat every meal, but I could enjoy some of it if it's around. I'd like to have pizza too. And some burgers. I wonder if he'll have that sort of layout for the house dinner?"

"Who knows with him." And that was the truth. Locke was a doctor now and knew the value of eating well. So did his wife, Alex. But he'd noticed that they could pig out on different foods, too, when it was around. "I have work to be done. Do you need anything else from me while you're here?"

"Are you shoving me out the door?" He said that he was actually because he really did have a lot of work to do. "All right, I see how you are. I'll get going, but I did want to ask you about the strip mall. Do you have anyone who wants to rent out one or more of the spaces? Have you heard anything?"

"Nothing other than the tire shop that's going to be going in as soon as his part of the building is finished. I've been wondering about a hardware store. We could certainly use one of those on that end of town, but I haven't heard anything. There was interest in a fishing shop, they'd sell licenses and such along with bait, but I've not heard anything more from them since they first asked. That would be great around here, I think. I would love to learn how to fish again. Remember doing that as kids?"

"Yes, sometimes it was the difference between us eating or not. I hated it." He said he had as well, but would really like to go out and fish again for fun.

"I don't know. You do it and let me know. I might even join you sometime. But my first thought is no, I want nothing to do with catching fish and having them because that's all there is."

"I understand." He thought that he did too. There were lots of things that he loved doing now that he hadn't as a teenager. There was chopping wood for his house that he used to do because it afforded them school supplies. Now it was fun for him to sit next to this fireplace and be warmed by wood that he'd cut up. There were other things, too, that he now enjoyed that he'd not as a child growing up with nothing. Less than nothing really.

Every once in a while, he'd think about his father. He was a mean bastard and a drunk. When they were growing up, his dad would be drunk before noon, and he was a mean drunk, too. Once, when he was bringing in the groceries that they had gotten, his dad was pissed off because they didn't buy any beer. Not that any of them were old enough to purchase the stuff for him, but he beat them all within an inch of their lives that night. It had been three days before any of them could walk around, and by then all the food was gone. He either ate it all while they were down or tossed it out. More than likely the latter of the two. Their father wasn't a good man at all.

"I'm headed out. I'll see you Thursday for

sure." He'd see him tomorrow, too, because that's just the way that they were. They would hang out together every day for some time, and it was good for them all. He loved his brothers more than anyone in the world, and he told them that daily.

They were close, the six of them, and even though they had wives now, most of them anyway, they were still close. He loved the fact that they got together once a week to hang out, and he loved even more that they saw each other daily when they were doing something as a family. Knox simply loved being around his family, no matter what was going on.

Chapter 5

Elaine had a good first week of school. She'd been able to get their names straight on the first couple of days, and their seating chart was easy enough to remember after that. Today was the beginning of her second week, and she was having so much fun that she was giddy when she got home. The best part of her day was when they had spelling of the words they had to work on, and they were catching up well after having a sub for so long. Elaine had lunch duty today, so she was able to hang out with all the kids while they had their lunch. Her favorite part of the day.

Once her class was ready to go outside, her assistant took them out. She'd be on lunch duty until all the kids were fed, about another hour and a half. However, she didn't mind. It was a way for her to meet the other teachers while getting to know the upper grades of students as well. Just as she was taking a break to run to the bathroom, her cell phone rang. It was Knox.

"You're working, so I'll keep this short. You owe me dinner. I was wondering if you were busy tonight." She told him she had papers to grade, but that wouldn't take her all that long to do. "Good. I'll pick you up at five, and we'll have a nice dinner at the *Crockery Pot*. My brother owns it, but he's not cooking tonight, so we might have some fun."

"Is your brother not fun?" He laughed and said that he was, but he could also be intrusive as well. "I see. All right, I'll see you then. I have to finish up my day here, and then I'll be ready at five for you."

"Great." He rang off, and she put her phone back in her pocket. They frowned upon you using your phone while in the classroom, but it was all right to use it in the hallway. She'd never abuse that rule and would keep it to a minimum. She was glad that Knox didn't keep her on the phone all that long, as she was sure he understood that she needed to keep her job.

By the time she got home, it was a quarter to five. There had been a meeting after classes were let out, and she'd had to attend. Then David, as he insisted that she call him, cornered her and asked her if she was doing all right. For some reason, he was starting to get on her nerves, and she didn't like that. He was creepy, too, the way he tried to stand close to her when he was talking to her. She noticed that he didn't do it to the other teachers when they were talking to him.

When her doorbell rang at five o'clock, she was finished getting dressed and was ready to go. She'd been looking forward to this all day and was excited to be able to spend more time with Knox. He was a funny guy, and she loved hanging out with him. He'd given her a lot of help when he'd helped her move her things into her place. Now she had a table and chairs as well as a couch to sit on. Things were moving quite nicely for her, and she couldn't be happier.

The Pot was busy, yet they were seated right away. He must have made reservations for them, and she was glad. She was hungry and couldn't wait to be seated. As soon as they were settled in their seats, bread and butter were brought out for them to munch on, and she was glad. The bread was a good appetizer as well as something to tide her over until they could order their meals.

She ordered the salmon with the rice pilaf and salad, and he ordered a steak with French fries and a salad. When their salads were brought to them, he took off his croutons, and she did the same for the cucumbers. They both traded what they didn't want to eat, and it worked out well. The house dressing was delicious.

"This is nice for our first date." She asked him if he thought that there would be more than this one. "I hope so. I've been looking forward to your calling me for our date since the night that you said you owed me. When you didn't call, I did, and I'm glad that I did."

"I am as well. However, I don't know about this

going any further than tonight. You're well out of my league." He laughed so hard that she could see tears in his eyes from it. "I'm serious. You're the wealthy Ericksons, and I'm a lowly school teacher who was barely making it when you came by to help me out. You should be dating people more in your tax bracket."

"I don't want to date anyone in my tax bracket, as you called it. I want to date you. You make me laugh, and I enjoy talking to you. You've been a good friend too, and I'm glad to have gotten to know you." She pointed out again how wealthy he was. "It's just money. It doesn't define me. I'll admit that it does have its perks, but I do want to see you again and again. Besides, you're not a lowly anything. Teachers are the ones who make our future what it will become, and I'm proud to know you."

Just as they were being asked if they wanted dessert, Knox took her hand into his. She didn't pull away like she thought she should have, but allowed him to hold her hand. Elaine thought him to be a romantic and was glad that they had this time together. When he figured out she wasn't the person for him, she was going to be heartbroken and decided that she was going to get as much as she could from the relationship while it lasted. Just as their desserts were being put on the table between them, David came out of nowhere and sat down at the table with them.

"What do you think you're doing?" She didn't know what to say to him as he was drawing unwanted attention to them. "You're mine, and you're not to be going out with anyone else."

"I don't know what you're talking about." He actually growled at her. When she tried to pull her hand away from Knox, he held her firmly and didn't let her go. "I'm out on a date. There is nothing that says I can't date while I'm working for the school. And as far as being yours, I have no idea where you got that idea. I belong to no one." He told her again that she was his.

"I will allow you this one time because I've not made myself clear when it came to you. When we were interviewing, there was a spark, and I've since decided that you'd be the perfect match for me." She asked him if he was married. "I am. But she doesn't have to know about us. And there will be an us, Elaine darling. Because it's what I want."

"I want you to leave." She looked over at Knox, who had told him again to leave. "You're disrupting our plans, and if you don't, I'm going to call the police."

"Call them. I'll just tell them that she's not working out, and I came here to fire her. See what that does for her money coming in." She decided that she'd had enough and was actually afraid of the principal now that he was showing his true side. Standing up, so did Knox; he never let go of her hand while they were standing either. "Where do you think you're going? I'm not nearly finished talking with you. You there, you're an Erickson. You know that she's only seeing you because you have money, don't you? All women are like that."

"I think you've said enough." Knox pulled out his cell phone only to have it knocked away by David. When she handed him hers, he tried to do the same, but was unable in his attempt to do so. Almost as soon as he called the police, they were coming into the restaurant. "I'm pressing charges against this man for knocking my cell phone away and interrupting our dinner. Not to mention he embarrassed my date."

It wasn't much, but it was enough to get him taken out of the restaurant. She sat down and tried to calm her nerves when Knox asked her if she was all right. She stared at him for several minutes before she could answer.

"I'm sorry about this." He asked her what for. "I've been thinking he's been creepy for the last week. Then today, he stood too close to me and had me backed up against the wall. I felt dirty when I got home and had to take a shower. That's why I was late in getting ready."

"I'll take care that he doesn't bother you again." She asked him how he was going to do that when he was her boss. "I don't know, but I'll do what I can. Are you sure you want to work for him after this? I mean, he seems a little unhinged if you ask me."

"I think he's more than a little unhinged, but I think I can handle him. If he gets too bad, well, I guess I'll have to quit. I won't allow him to hurt me like he has tonight and get away with it." She thought about what he'd said about her belonging to him. "I don't know what he meant by that. I mean, we've never even had a personal conversation since I've been working there."

"As we said, he's unhinged. I'm going to do a more extensive background check on him when I get home. I can't believe that I haven't done it before now. I guess I just assumed that one had been done on him before he'd been hired. I'll make sure I dig deep, too." She played around with her dessert, no longer interested in it as she'd been before. "Have a bite or two, and I'll take you home. I'm worried about you if you want to know the truth. Just be extra careful at school tomorrow. There is no telling what he'll do when he has you all to himself."

"I'll be careful." She would too. There wouldn't be any more cornering her either. She was going to stand up for herself. And for as much as she needed the job, she wouldn't hesitate to quit if it came to that. "You be careful too. He's already shown that he isn't above making a scene about this, so you make sure that you keep an eye out for him as well."

"I will." Knox ended up paying the check with the comment that he'd have to have another date with her because she would still owe him. As they walked out to his car, he held her hand tightly in his much larger one, and when they got to the car, he pulled her into his arms. The kiss was more than she could have hoped for, and when he lifted his head, he smiled at her. "I've been wanting to do that all evening. Since I picked you up."

"You're very sure of yourself, aren't you?" He laughed and told her if only that were true. "I like you, Knox. And could easily fall in love with you if you keep being a gentleman like you are."

"Good. Then my plan is working." He held the door open for her until she was inside his car. Then he walked around to his side and got in. "How about we get together on Saturday? I have a meeting first thing in the morning, but after that I'm free all day. We could go to town and have a nice walk around again without David hanging around to pounce on us."

"I'd like that very much." He kissed the back of her hand, and she wanted to sing to the world that she'd met a nice man. It wasn't often that a nice man would come around to date her, but with him, she really could fall in love with him and never look back.

But as she'd told him, he was out of her league when it came to them going beyond seeing each other on occasion.

By the time they were pulling up in front of her place, she'd convinced herself that this was going to be a one-time thing. He was just being nice about asking her out again, and that this would be the end of things. However, when he walked her to her door and kissed her goodnight, she was nearly to the point where she wanted to beg him to see her again.

Sitting down at her makeshift desk, the table that had been delivered yesterday, she figured out her finances. She wasn't going to have a lot extra with her checks coming in regularly now, but she could make it until her lease ran out. Writing out her resignation, she was finished with it at midnight. There was no way that she was going to be able to work for the school again with David around. Sending it to the board before she changed her mind, she went to bed with a heavy heart. She loved her job but wasn't going to be subject to David any more than she had to.

Living in a small town like this one, it would be all over town what had happened at the *Pot*. By this time tomorrow night, everyone would know, and she'd have to live with it until she could move on. David had messed with the wrong girl if he thought that he could get by with treating her like he had.

She wanted to call Knox and tell him what she'd done, but it was late, and she didn't want him to tell her how crazy she'd been in quitting. Not that she thought that he would, but she didn't know him well enough to know what he'd say to her. The man was wealthy and still worked. How much would he make fun of her if she were to tell him that, without a steady income, she was going to be eating light over the next few months because she was nearly broke?

She didn't sleep well. She would think about David and the way that he looked at her and be frightened all over again. He'd not hurt her in any way, but she thought that he might well have if they'd been alone. And that scared her more than anything. The lengths that he'd go to in order to make her his. Shivering at the thought, she was up well before the alarm went off and was ready to go an hour before she had to be at the school. She did wonder how long it would take before the board notified him of her resignation, but wasn't going to worry about that now. She had a full day's work ahead of her, and she was going to do her best to make it one of the best days she'd had.

~*~

Knox found three different incidents of things that had happened with David Sheen. He'd been fired from his last job for beating up a woman teacher for her being married. That was his excuse. When he'd been asked why he'd done it, he said that she wouldn't leave her husband for him, and that was enough of an excuse for him. The woman recovered but didn't teach anymore.

The other two were of the same thing but different schools. And he'd not beaten anyone up. David had been to nine different schools in the last eleven years, and he wondered what the reason was that he'd left the other six. As much as he dug into his life, the more he wondered if anyone else had been hurt by him. He sent a letter to the board to let them know that they had a serial troublemaker in their school. He wondered what they'd do about it.

Getting ready for work the next morning, he heard from two of the nine board members as well. He'd been told that one of the teachers had given their two weeks' notice as well, and was asked if it had anything to do with David. He asked if it was Elaine, and he was proud of her for not going back to the school. It wouldn't bode well for her, he had a feeling, and didn't want her hurt.

They asked him why it was just coming to light, and he told them that he had assumed that they'd done a thorough background check on him when they hired him. They said that they didn't know if one had been done or not, and that pissed him off. Why weren't they doing these on everyone that they hired, but they didn't have an answer. Well, he was going to take care of it now and told them that they needed to fire him before he hurt someone else. They agreed and asked him to do it.

"No. I've got a job, and that's all there is to it. He's working today with Elaine and will more than likely hurt her if she tries to get away from him. Or if he figures out that she's going to be quitting. You haven't told him yet, have you?" They hadn't, thank goodness, but that didn't mean he wouldn't find out sooner rather than later. "I understand that, but he's going to hurt her if he gets the chance. You have to do something now before it's too late, and you have a lawsuit on your hands about her. This time, he might not settle for just beating her up. He might well kill her then, where will you be?"

"We'll go over and talk to him immediately. We'll tell him what you told us and then fire him. We just don't need this sort of thing going on at that level of school." He didn't think that needed this going on at any level, but he kept his mouth shut. They were going to fire him, and that was about the best news he'd heard all day.

Perhaps then they'd hire Elaine back, and she'd be able to stick around so that he could see her again. Laughing to himself, he was happy that he'd not told them that when he'd been thinking about it. That would have been something that they wouldn't have found so funny as he did.

By noon, it was all over town about what had happened last night at the restaurant. There was even a video from someone who had recorded it. He watched it three times before sending it off to the board. The one thing that he'd not heard about was the firing of David. He hoped they didn't change their mind. But since he wasn't on the board like one of his brothers was, he'd get with Locke to see what he could find out.

He found it hard to focus on his work. He worried about Elaine and David through most of the morning. When he was called by the board, them telling him that they'd had to arrest David for not wanting to leave, he knew that it would be all over town again about that. He just wanted to hear from Elaine to make sure she was doing all right before he could concentrate on his work.

At lunch, he called her. When it went straight to voicemail, he was nervous that something had happened. Almost as soon as he closed the connection with her phone, it rang back. He knew the number was hers, but the voice wasn't. It was Locke, and he sounded stressed.

"How much do you know about Elaine Westcock?" He asked him what had happened. "She's on her way to the emergency room. They found her in the parking lot this morning, beaten to shit. They figured that she'd been out there since eight this morning." It was nearly noon now, and he pulled his coat on and was headed to the door. "She's been beaten up. I won't know anything until I see her. You want to tell me how well you know her? I've seen the video of the two of you on a date last night."

"I'm in love with her." He'd not said that out loud before, but knew it was right. "I think I have been since I first met her."

"Come into the emergency department, and I'll take care that she gets the best of care." He thanked his big brother. "All's well. I'll see her, then I'll have to turn it over to another doctor. I can't see someone that would be related to me, you understand."

"I do, and I thank you. I'm on my way now." He had to stop the car when he nearly pulled out into traffic at the end of his driveway. Taking in a deep breath, he was ready to go again when he felt calmer. Christ, all he needed to do was get himself in the emergency department while she lay there in pain. He was pulling in when the ambulance was pulling away.

He couldn't see her right away because he wasn't related to her. He wanted to scream at the people at the desk when they told him that. It wasn't until he saw Locke that things started to go his way. He was back in the room with her as soon as Locke led him back.

"She's been given pain medication. When she woke up, she was coherent and knew where she was. But since they gave her something for the pain that she's in, she's been sleeping off and on. I'm going to have her taken to get a C-scan while she's out. It'll be easier on her. You stay in this room and wait for her so that no one causes you any trouble." He said that he would. "Knox, she's been beaten to shit, and she told the police who had done it. I worry that she's been out there for so long. I'm going to make sure she gets the best care we can give her."

"Thanks." He sat down in the chair and took her hand into his. It was black and blue, too, as was her face. There were a lot of cuts on her that he knew would need stitches. Her lip was swollen too, and he could see that her eye was on the way to swelling shut soon. His heart hurt for her, and he gently kissed the back of her hand. "Oh, Elaine, I'm so sorry that this has happened to you."

When the transporter came to get her, he wanted to tell him that he was going too. But he remembered his warning from Locke and stayed put. All he could think about was that someone had beaten her up for no other reason than she'd said no to them. As soon as she was gone for about twenty minutes, the police showed up to talk to her. He told them where she was.

"You're the man from last night." He said that

he was and that he'd had no idea that the man would go this far. "Neither did we when we spoke to him this morning at the school. He never mentioned that he'd encountered her in the parking lot. Another teacher had seen her, or there is no telling how much longer she would have been out there in the rain."

"David has been fired from what I was told." He said that he had been, and they had escorted him out of the building. "Elaine works there, so I did worry that he'd try something when she was there, but I never expected him to beat her up. This isn't the first time that he's done something like this. There was another teacher who he beat up badly as well. She had to stop teaching; she was so afraid after that."

"I'm to understand that she's given her notice too. That might have set him off a bit, too. If what he said about her belonging to him is true, then there is no telling how that would affect him when she told him." He said that as far as he knew, David didn't know that she'd given her notice. The board had said that they'd not do that. "Good for them. They might well have saved her life if he thought that she was no longer going to be in his sights."

When Elaine came back, she was awake but in a great deal of pain. The officer who seemed to be in charge asked her if she could talk to them, and even though she said that she could, he was still worried.

Holding her hand, he knew that when she squeezed his hand, she was hurting. He only hoped that they'd not ask too many questions so that she could get some pain medications again for her injuries. And she had a lot of them.

She was able to get what she needed after the police left. She dozed in and out for a while, telling him what had happened to her in the parking lot. How like last night, he'd come out of nowhere and had knocked her around with a bat. When she cried, he hurt for her and wanted to find David and beat him to death. It wouldn't do anyone any good, but he knew he'd feel better about things if he could show him what it was like to beat on someone smaller than him.

When Locke came to talk to them, Elaine was awake and hurting again. After getting her enough to take the edge off, he told them what he'd been able to find so far. She had a concussion as well as a broken wrist. There were marks on her back that worried him, so he was going to run more tests. What concerned him the most was the wounds to her head. There were three of them that had been knocked into her, and Locke said that she'd have to be careful when moving around in the bed. He was sure there was more, but he didn't ask. The little bit that he'd told them was enough to have him angry at David enough to go out and find him.

It was midnight when they decided to put her

into a room. She'd been sick once, and Locke said that was normal for a head injury. The bruises on her body were getting darker the longer she lay there, and her eyes were both swollen shut. Her lips weren't doing any better than her eyes, but at least she could speak around them. Holding her hand for as long as she'd let him, he stayed with her when they moved her to her own room.

He didn't take his eyes off her all night. He did doze a bit off and on, but would wake every time she moved. Locke had gotten her another doctor because of the relationship that was going on between the two of them, but he checked in on her when he could, and he loved him for that. As soon as the morning came around, she was taken down for more tests. He hated not being with her, but he knew, too, that she was in good hands while she was here. He hoped so at least.

His brothers came by one at a time while she was gone. He wondered if Locke had set that up for him so he'd not be so overwhelmed. And he was too. His need to do something for her was making him crazy, and all he wanted to do was to make sure that she was going to be all right. It wasn't until the afternoon that Zander came in that he knew anything about David.

"He's been arrested without bail. He'll have to wait for the judge to come back around before he'll be given a bail amount, if he gets any at all." He asked if he'd said anything about why he'd hurt her. "Only that she was his and that she didn't want anything to do with him. His wife has left him, too. I know that I would have had I been in her shoes. I think from what I've heard, she's gone to see her mother. Might be the best thing for her to distance herself from him as far as she can."

"He lost his job at the school, too. I spoke to the board this morning. Or yesterday. I have no idea what day this is." Zander told him. "So it's been a whole day since he took his anger out on her. I wonder if he had any plans for me."

"I didn't hear if he had or not, but you still need to be careful. You don't need to end up lying next to her during the time that she needs you." He told Zander that he'd fallen in love with her. "Yeah, I figured as much. When it happens for us, it's quick. I just hope that when I find someone to love, they're as nice and good for me as the rest of you have been. I need a woman in my life to keep me on the straight and narrow."

When Zander left, he stayed with Elaine. She was still getting pain medications that were making her in and out of things, but she would talk to him when she could. He told her that he'd fallen in love with her, and she cried. He wasn't sure if that was a good thing or not, but his heart was hers no matter how she felt about him.

Chapter 6

Elaine had seventy-four stitches in her head, with all three wounds. And more than that, throughout her body. She'd been dragged across the parking lot a couple of times when he'd tried to get her to his car. Also, she had a cast on her wrist. The rest of her body felt like it had gone a few rounds with a fighter, and she knew that to be true. Since she couldn't see out of her eyes, she had to wonder what she looked like right now. She'd bet that it wasn't pretty.

"I have your lunch here, Elaine. It's not much, just some broth, but the doctor said you were to eat as much of it as you could when you could." She said that she'd try. "That's my girl."

She couldn't understand that every time she woke up, Knox was here. Not that she'd ask him that. She loved that he was here for her when she woke up from a nightmare. He would soothe her to the point where she was feeling better, then talk to her about what was going on around the town. Never mentioning David or what had happened at the school lot. She loved him for that. Finally getting up the nerve, she asked him why he was spending so much time with her.

"You want me to be honest?" She said that she didn't want him to lie to her. It wouldn't be a good friendship if he lied to her about something like this. "I've fallen in love with you. I don't know if it's the forever kind of love, I believe it is, but since I've never been in love before, I have no way of knowing. But I do love you. With all my heart."

"You don't know me that well." He said he understood that too and knows that he didn't. "But you still say that you love me."

"I do. Very much so." He took her injured hand into his and kissed her fingers. "You're right, I don't know you well, but I find that I want to know you. I want to know all about you and what you did growing up. You make me want to be with you all the time because when I'm not with you, I'm thinking about being with you. Understand?"

"No. You are a very wealthy man, Knox. Not the sort of man who hangs out with teachers. Well, I guess I'm an ex-teacher now. Did I tell you that I turned in my resignation? I'm sure after this, they've accepted it." He said that, as far as the board was concerned, she was still a teacher at the kindergarten level. "I don't understand that either. I guess I will have to wait until I'm better before I'm able to figure things out for myself."

She put up her hand to touch Knox and felt his face beneath her fingers. He had shaved, his mustache just beneath her fingertips. She could feel the smoothness of his cheeks and nose. His hair, a bit long, curled around her fingers, and she held them. Elaine could almost see him since she knew what he looked like and wanted to tell him that she loved him, too.

"You're thinking very hard." She told him then how much she'd fallen in love with him as well. "Good. We're halfway there as far as I'm concerned. I wish that I could kiss you, but I know that you'd be in a great deal of pain if I did."

"He really did this to me." He asked her what he'd said when he was knocking her around. "That I belonged to him and no one else. I didn't understand that part. I never belonged to anyone before. Then he said that I was a whore and a slut. That I wasn't worthy enough to be his mistress. He actually called me his mistress and said how I'd messed things up between us—meaning him and me. I never had a clue that he felt that way about me. Then, when I told him no, he trapped me between my open car door and the parking lot and started hitting me with a bat. At some point, he told me that he was taking me home, and I remember him dragging me across the parking lot."

"Oh, baby, I'm so sorry that I wasn't there to help you, but like you said, since you've never felt that way about him, there was no way to know that he was going to do that to you." She told him how she thought of him when she was being beaten and wished that he could have been there for her. "You've no idea how much I wish I could have been there with you right then. I would have protected you. And I will from now on. Protect you with my life."

"He might well have hurt you, too. I keep thinking about how he approached us during dinner. How he was so angry then. What kind of person does that to someone they barely know? I certainly never had any feelings toward him in that way at all." Knox said that he'd done some digging on him and found out some things. He told her what he'd been able to find. "So he's done this before, and the board didn't do anything about it? Christ, no wonder he did it if he got away with it the first time. I should sue the school for allowing him to be there when he should have been in jail or prison."

"I told them this might well happen. You should do it. With them not doing a background check on him at all, things would come up later with him. His wife left him, too, and took their children. I can only hope that he treated his family better than he treated you. I can't imagine what was going through his head when he was beating you to shit." She asked him if Zander would do it for her. "If he doesn't, I will. I tried to tell them when they hired the teachers that they had to do extensive background checks on everyone. It only takes a few minutes if you know how to do it."

When her lunch tray was taken away, she was told that she'd eaten all of it. The staff were being so kind in telling her things when they were in the room. Since she couldn't see anything, it didn't startle her as badly when one of them touched her. The doctor told her that it would be another couple of weeks before the swelling would go down enough that they could see if there was any damage to her eyes. She hoped not. There was enough going on with her body as it was. She reached for Knox again, and he took her hand again.

"What plans do you have when you get out of here? You're not going to be able to be alone with your sight gone right now." She said that she'd just stumble around her place until she got the pattern of it down. "I was going to suggest you stay with me. I have plenty of room, and I can keep an eye on you while you're up and around. There wouldn't be any pressure for you to be careful either. I have furniture, but not a lot. I like the sparseness of the house."

"What about sleeping arrangements? I don't know that I'd be any good in bed right now. I'm usually sorest at night." He said she could have the master bedroom, and he'd sleep in one of the others. "I'll do it. But only if the doctor thinks that I shouldn't be left at home alone. I don't want to put you out. I know you offered, but that doesn't mean that you want to be nursemaid to someone that can't see and is as banged up as much as I am."

"I would love you to live with me even if you had your sight and weren't banged up. I love you." She wished that she could see him, to see if he was making fun of her or not. Not that she thought he would, but she was so insecure right now that anything made her feel like she was being teased. "I don't know if you'll believe me or not, but I think you're beautiful right now. I'm profoundly grateful that he didn't kill you when he was beating you."

"I am as well." She felt tears rolling down her cheeks, and he begged her not to cry as it was breaking his heart. "The first time that someone tells me he loves me and I can't get a kiss, nor can I see if he's revolted by my looks."

"I told you, you're beautiful. I wish you didn't hurt so much, but I think that after a few more days you'll see that your swelling will go down and you'll be able to peek at me." She laughed. "There's my girl. I knew that you'd be able to see the bright side of things once I got you in the mood. And you are beautiful. I think you're the most courageous person that I've ever met. Not many people would have been able to go through what you have and still have a sense of humor like you do. I love that about you, too."

"And I love you too." She lay back on the bed and thought about where she was and what was going on around her. "It's been weird not having been able to see things. I swear to you that I can smell things better. Not a good thing when you're in a hospital. I can also hear the nurses out at the desk sometimes at night. They talk low so I can't understand them, but I do hear them. Since I'm not eating anything really, I don't know if my taste buds are any better. But I'm betting that they would be if my mouth wasn't so sore."

"The doctor said you'd have to see your dentist after you heal a bit more. Some of your teeth had been hit with the ball bat, and it might cause them to be loose." She made a mental note to call him when she got out of here. "You've lost both earrings in your right ear. They're both in your left, but they removed those when they cleaned your wounds."

"There is so much wrong with me, it's small wonder that I don't want to see myself." He asked her if she wanted anything from her home. "Nothing there. I was thinking about some of the papers that I needed to grade, but I wouldn't be able to do that either."

"I'll run them into the school so that someone can grade them for you. Also, is there anything that was in your backpack that needs to be returned to the school? The police have it, but said that I can pick it up for you at any time." She said that it had a couple of credit cards in it as well as her driver's license. "I'll make sure that they're still in there if you give me permission to look."

"Yes, of course. That would be wonderful. I hope no one has been having a good time on them. They have a good limit, but I can't afford to run the bill up too much." He said he'd take care of that for her. "Have we talked about this before? I have a feeling that you've been telling me things for the last few days that I just never got."

"It's been all right. I don't mind reminding you again." So he had been repeating himself for her. What a lovely thing to do. "There are some other things that you need to be made aware of. You've pressed charges against the school and David separately. The school for no having working cameras, and of course, you understand why David would be done separately. Zander did that for you when you were first hurt. It's kept David in jail until such time as the judge comes around to hear what he has to say."

"What do you think that he's going to plead? I mean, it's obvious that he hurt me." He told her how he'd called her cell phone when she had not shown up to work on time. "You're kidding me? Even though he'd put me in a position to not be there on time? The bastard. I wish I could see him now. I believe I got in a few punches of my own."

"You did. He has a broken nose and his wrist, like yours, is broken. He had to have forty-four stitches to his head where they think you slammed him with the door." She asked how no one noticed that. "They did, but he said that he'd had a fender bender on the way to work and had cut himself on the door getting out. The medic who took care of him said that it would have had to have hurt badly to be hit where he was. Just at the corner of his right eye."

She would doze in and out throughout the day. Sometimes she'd wake startled out of her sleep and know that she'd been dreaming about the beating she'd taken. Knox was forever there, and she was grateful for his comforting hand on hers. She, however, wanted him to go home to get some rest because they both knew that he wasn't sleeping all that well here at the hospital. Of course, he'd told her no, that he was all right. She threatened him, and he finally said he'd go home and shower.

"You need to rest, too. You're not going to be able to help me if you're sick. I need you to be strong for me. I might need you sometime, and if you're ill or something, what will I do?" He said he would take a nap. "Good. I'll feel better when you do. I know that I need a nap now and again with all the pain medication that they're giving me. I wish they didn't, but sometimes my body hurts so bad that I want to crawl into a corner and suck my thumb. If I didn't hurt so much getting down there, I might well do it."

After about an hour, she had no concept of time nowadays. He said that he was going to leave her. When he kissed her on the forehead, careful of the wounds there, she held tightly to his hand. It was all she could offer him, the way that she was feeling, and she loved that he didn't make fun of her when she did it.

As soon as he left, she wanted to call him back. The room was too quiet, and she didn't have anyone in the room to make the quiet more tolerable. Just as her dinner was being brought in, she thought of Knox and how he would tell her what he was feeding her with each spoonful. Feeling sorry for herself, she did the best she could without having any idea what she'd been eating or if she got any of it on her gown.

She cried herself to sleep once and woke to someone in the room. Not having any idea, she cried out when the person touched her. Then he told her that he was Locke, that Knox had called him to tell him to watch over her.

"That was nice of him. I sent him home to get a shower and a nap. I don't know if he'll take a nap or not, but I know that he needs it." Locke said that he was lying down when he talked to him. "Well, that's good. He won't do himself any good to be sick when I need him."

"You've fallen in love with him, haven't you?" She asked him if he was going to tell her to back off. "Why would I do that? He's a grown man, and you're a grown woman. I'm surprised that it's taken him so long to tell you. I could tell that he loved you when he was talking about helping you move into your place."

"That seems so far away now." He said it had been about a month. "I've tried to tell him he could do better, but he won't listen to me."

"You could do better, too, but I think the two of you make the perfect couple. You'll do him some good, and I think he'll do the same for you." She told him that he was kind to her. "He'd better be. Any one of us would kick his ass if he's not." The two of them laughed, and she felt better about him being there. "We're very close, the six of us and our wives have just made it better between us. I hope you'll be a part of the family soon."

She hoped so as well. When the nurse came in to take her blood pressure, she was also asked if she wanted anything for pain. She didn't because she was feeling better daily and didn't want to make a habit of the medications. She'd be out soon and couldn't wait to be on her own two feet. Tomorrow, she was supposed to start walking the hallways to get herself in better shape. She hoped that her gown was closed up tight, as she couldn't see what it looked like.

~*~

Knox woke up and couldn't believe that he'd slept all night. He felt horrible for not being there if Elaine had needed him. Taking another shower and getting dressed, he had to admit that he felt better. He'd been running low for the last few days, and it had finally caught up with him. Talking to Locke, he said that he'd left her at midnight when she was sleeping well and came back in the morning to help her with her breakfast.

"I wonder how she can eat so little of this stuff and survive. It's just soft stuff that looks like baby food. I never realized that when I put someone on a soft diet." He said that she was on liquids before, so she was glad that she'd been upgraded. "She's excited to be able to walk around the halls today, but I warned her to be careful that she doesn't get dizzy. She's been in bed for a week now, and she might not be very steady on her feet."

"I'll remind her of that when I see her." He told him to take his time, that he had this. "I know, but I miss her. Christ, why didn't anyone tell me that love was all-consuming? It's like I can't breathe without thinking about what she might be doing."

"I'm so glad that you found someone to love, little brother. It is the best feeling in the world." He agreed with him. "And to think we all thought that you and Carrie would be an item. I'm glad you were able to find Elaine when you did. It's nice to be able to add to the family. I wish that Martha were here. Wouldn't she be getting a kick out of all of us finding someone to love?"

"She'd be as happy as we are for us." Locke said that he agreed with him and told him how much he missed her daily. "I do as well. I will think of something that I want to tell her, and be sad when I remember that she's gone. For as little time as we had with her, she certainly made a huge impact on our lives. And I don't just mean the money, I mean in our actual lives."

"She was the best." He had to agree with him about that. Martha had helped shape them into the men that they are today. And she'd loved them. No one had loved them up until they came into her life. If not for a broken-down van that died in front of her house, there was no telling what sort of lives they might have lived. "I can't believe she's been gone almost a year now. It doesn't seem possible. Does it?"

"Not at all." Knox told his brother how he still goes out to her gravesite and talks to her. "I think that we all do that in some way, talk to her. Like we said, she was a huge part of our lives for so little time we had with her. Knowing that she was there for us, too, made any decisions we made all that much more important to us. Because she approved of them."

"She loved us no matter if our decisions were good or bad. Though I don't think that there were all that many bad decisions we made when we got out of the house that we grew up in. Do you ever think of our father?" He said he did on occasion. "I do as well. Not to dwell on his life, but I was never so happy to get away from him as I was that day."

They decided to just leave home with the shirts on their backs because had they taken something their father would have accused them of stealing from him and had them arrested. Locke had bought the van second-hand and had kept it hidden away until the day they left. Since he'd been at a friend's house playing chess, they one by one got into the van until he was ready to leave. To this day, Knox wondered how they'd been able to make such a clean break of things and leave their father. He'd been an abusive bastard to them since they were small children. It was a wonder how they'd been able to survive him all those years.

"Do you suppose he missed us?" He said that he more than likely did miss them because they were the only ones working. "For years after we left, I wanted to go to him and see why he hated us so much. I never did, but I do wonder at times." Locke shook his head before speaking.

"The only time he was remotely nice to us was when there was someone around, like the police, mostly. It's a right shame that the police department knew us all by name because of him. I don't ever want to be compared to him. I never want anything associated with him to come back and bite us in the ass. I don't think that it will, but I think about that sometimes." Knox said that he used to think about him finding them when they first moved here. "I think we all did like when we'd have money on us. I'd think that he was going to come out of nowhere and beat us for the cash. But he's dead now, and nothing we have to worry about."

"That's true." Knox smiled then. "I couldn't point him out in a line-up if it ever was to have come to that. He is nothing but a blimp in my mind. Someone who means nothing to me and never will again. I'm glad that he sired us, but that's the extent of anything that I've felt for him in a long time."

"You got that right." When Locke left him with Elaine, she had to go and have some x-rays done. They were doing them every other day to make sure that she was healing correctly. With tomorrow being her first day of walking around, they wanted to make sure that she wasn't going to harm herself when she did it. He couldn't wait for her to be up and around. He loved that she was getting better daily.

When Elaine went to sleep, he pulled out his laptop and worked on a few things that he'd been putting off in order to stay with her. There were quite a few emails that he'd had to answer, but he decided that he could put them off for another day. Tomorrow was going to be a big day, and he wanted to be rested. Since he'd been home, they'd brought him in another chair that was actually comfortable, and he decided to keep up with his sleep. Once he was laid back in the chair, he closed his eyes. Like Elaine, he could hear the nurses talking out at the desk but could not make out what they were saying. It was a calming way to get some sleep, and he dozed off quickly.

After a breakfast of pureed foods, she wanted to get up and get around. It took the staff three times to get her out of bed. She was dizzy and was glad that Locke had warned them of that. Once she was up, she held onto the bed and walked around the room for a little while before she became tired and needed to rest. Taking it easy was the advice of the doctor who had seen her, and he was happy with her first day getting around. Tomorrow, he promised them it would be better.

Elaine was disappointed. She imagined herself walking the halls by now. He was sort of happy that she wasn't. If she'd fallen while walking, there was no telling what more damage she would have done to herself. It was scary to think that she'd only been in bed for a week and was so weak. He was going to make sure that she rested a great deal so that she'd not fall.

"I guess I should be happy with what I was able to do." He said that he was. "I don't know what I was thinking. I guess that I'd get out of bed and walk. I did a lot of walking before being hurt. I think that I thought I'd be in good enough shape to do it again."

"I'm just glad that you didn't fall. You could have." She told him that she thought that she might have too, that she'd been so dizzy and weak that she was glad for something to hold onto while up. "Tomorrow, they said they'd get you a walker. I'd use it if I were you. Just so you have something to hang onto while up and about."

"I'd feel so old." He laughed, and she stuck her tongue out at him. "Well, first of all, I guess since I can't see, that it'll be fine, but it still bothers me that I'm not as strong as I thought that I might be."

"Remember too that you've not been eating all that much either. There can't be that many calories in what you're consuming." She said that she'd never thought of that. "When you get stronger, I'm betting that your doctor will allow you more food that isn't as mushy as the stuff you've been eating. I know you can taste how bland it is."

"It's not all that good, but it's something to put in my belly." He smiled, and she could almost feel his approval. "I want an apple so bad. Not applesauce. But an honest-to-goodness apple that I can bite into. I like applesauce all right, but it's not the same. This time of year, I make myself a can of caramel and have that with apples as a snack. Have you ever made your own caramel? It's super easy."

"No, I don't think that I have." She told him how to do it. "That does sound very easy. Just simmer a can of sweetened condensed milk for four hours, and that makes caramel? That sounds too easy."

"You have to make sure that the can is covered in water all the time. If you don't, then it could explode. I've heard of the mess hot caramel can make of a kitchen if you allow the can to get uncovered." Knox said he was going to make some when he got home. "Good. Maybe by next week, I'll be able to eat something more than just mushy food. You're going to love it. I know that I do."

They talked about the different kinds of foods that they liked. He loved food that was spicy, and she didn't care for it. While she told him that she could eat Mexican food every day, he said that his favorite was Chinese. They were teasing each other about the kinds of foods they both liked and were having a good time.

The nurse came in with her dinner tray just as she was saying how hungry she was. He went to the cafeteria to get himself something to eat so as not to tempt her with something that he got. After all the talk about food, he was nearly starving when he finally decided to have the special for the day, roast beef and noodles with sour cream. It was really good, but not like he got at home, but he was fine. It filled his belly, and that was the best part.

Chapter 7

David didn't understand why he was the only one in jail. Elaine had beat on him as well. Of course, he'd not been put in the hospital, but that didn't seem fair to him. He didn't much care for being in jail at all. It was going to mess up his chances of keeping his job.

He didn't care for being a principal at an elementary school. He didn't want to have to work at all, but there wasn't any way that he could afford his new house and his wife if he didn't work. She told him that she was going to be a stay-at-home mom, and that was final.

He wouldn't mind that job at all. Just hanging around the house all day doing nothing was something that he could get into. His wife told him that it wasn't as easy as he thought it was, but he knew better. She barely had to do anything all day but take care of their kids, and that wasn't all that hard. They never bothered him when he got home from work.

Elaine would have made a near-perfect mistress. She was a bit mouthy, but he could take care of that. A few hits to the mouth and she'd quit that stuff right now. He thought about the fact that she'd hit him back and wondered if that was going to be a habit with her. He didn't care for his mistress being mean to him. That shit just wasn't right.

He'd never had one before, a mistress. He'd read about them in all kinds of stories. The man would be pampered and catered to when he was with her, and he'd be a better husband to his wife. Of course, he thought he was god to his wife now. Never telling her how to do her job at home. All he expected was for dinner to be on the table when he was ready for it and to keep the house neat. Since it was forever neat anyway, he just figured that she'd be able to skip over that part of being pissed off at her and let her slide. For all he knew, she had someone come in and clean up after them. She was to be able to do the bills, too. David didn't want to mess with bills when he wanted to relax when he got home from work.

He knew that he made good money. There seemed to be enough for them to take a vacation every year. A nice one, too, where all he had to do was show up and have a good time. Again, she more than likely got someone to do that for them. He thought his wife was lazy as fuck and didn't understand when she harped on him about doing more around the house. He paid for it and all the food. The least she could do was mow the lawn when it was time and take out the trash can. He did bring it back up to the house when he was outside. What more did she want from him? Everything apparently.

Wondering how he could get his wife to pay for an apartment for his mistress—he loved the sound of that when he thought about it—without her pitching a bitch about spending money that they didn't have. She'd just have to make it work out, that was all, and when she did, he didn't want to hear about it again. He'd have to lay down the law.

Hitting his wife had never been anything that he did. He was tempted at times, just to pop her in the mouth when she started feeling like she was being taken advantage of. He didn't understand where that was coming from. He took care of her needs when he was in the mood. Here of late, he'd not been in the mood; he wanted Elaine. She was going to be his mistress as soon as he got her to take back this having him arrested and put in jail. It wasn't a good beginning for them when she'd done something like this to him.

David knew nothing about having affairs. He'd been afraid of his wife finding out. Well, now that she'd left him high and dry, he was willing to forget about what Elaine had done to him for a little extra pussy. He giggled when he thought of that word. It was one of the words he'd never allowed to be said in his life. That, nor the word fuck, except for the day that he'd taught Elaine a lesson.

Sitting on the side of his cot, he had to wonder who had taught whom a lesson. When she'd slammed his head into the car door, he'd been sure she was trying to kill him. He certainly had enough of a headache from what she'd done to him. And for what reason? He'd only been trying to teach her a lesson in going out with someone when he had not given her permission. That was one of the things that he'd read about mistresses, they weren't supposed to do shit without the man's permission.

Pretty on his arm when he had to go to functions was one of the things they were used for. Of course, something fresh to fuck, he giggled again. Elaine wasn't doing anything that she was supposed to do with him, and he wondered if he needed to make her a list of things she was allowed to do and not do. Right at the top of the list would be beating him back. That was for the birds, and it hurt too. There was never any mention of him being hurt by his mistress in any book that he'd ever read. And he'd read up on it a great deal.

"She is going to have to be nicer to me." He didn't like talking to himself, but since he was all alone and there wasn't anyone in the cells next to him, he could talk as much as he wanted. His head hurt too much to be thinking all the time, and that was her fault, too. "Did I make a mistake in thinking she'd make a good mistress?"

He didn't want to believe that. She was beautiful and smart. Someone with whom he could hold a conversation sometimes when he wanted to talk. He knew that she'd been in the service, which might account for her being able to get in a few blows of her own when he'd been trying to teach her a lesson. He was going to have to tell her not to use that stuff on him again. It was too painful and wasn't fair that she knew more about beating people up than he did. David was going to knock that right out of her head and soon.

He actually thought it would be nice to have someone that he could knock around when he was having a bad day. Just a few jabs to the face and he'd be in a better mood. Not, however, if she was going to be hitting him back all the time. As he'd said, it wasn't fair that she knew more about how to do moves than he did.

"You have a visitor. Did you want to see him here or in one of the rooms?" He said he could see him here; he was comfortable. "Well, just so you know, we record your cell too. So you'd better not say anything that might get you into trouble with the law. Mr. Erickson insisted on your knowing that right up front."

"You can't record me unless I say it's all right." He told him that it was one of the rules he was told about when he was brought in. "I don't care. I don't want anyone recording me when I'm having a—who is this person anyway? Why did he want to see me?"

"You knocked around his wife." After the man left him, he was still pondering who he'd knocked around that was someone's wife. The only person that he could remember in all his life was Elaine, and she had not been married. He knew that for a fact; it was on her application. When the man came down the hall, he had a chair with him, and David wished that he had one.

Sitting on his cot wasn't all that comfortable, nor did he like sleeping in the bed either. He wanted a nice desk, too, so that he could write up things when he thought of them. Thinking without notes had never been his strong point, and he wasn't sure how some people thought on their feet when he'd heard that odd saying.

"David." He said his name was Mr. Sheen. "You're in no position to tell me what I can call you or not. So I'll call you by your first name because it annoys you so much. I'm here to talk to you about Elaine. She and I are going to be married soon, and I wanted you to be the first to know."

"That's not possible. Not only that, but as my mistress, she won't be able to stay with you when I have her locked up in an apartment that I'm paying for." He asked him if he'd really lock her up. "Yes. She's not shown herself to be all that trustworthy when she's out and about. Dating you is just one example of how she's not playing fair when I'm going to be footing the bills for her. Of course, she'll have to be the one doing the bills. I don't want to be bothered with that."

"So you think she's going to want to be your mistress after you beat her to snot? I doubt there is anyone who would agree to be your anything after the way you treated Elaine. She certainly isn't going to be willing." He said that he'd have to pop her around a bit to get her to agree. "Pop her around a bit? The last time you did that, you nearly killed her. I heard that she got in a couple of good hits herself. Are you still pissing blood?"

"No, the doctor said that she'd damaged my kidney a bit when she kicked me. I won't allow her to do that again. She fights dirty." He nodded but didn't say anything else. "Why are you here other than to lie to me about having her as your wife? I'm going to keep her well as my mistress, and there will be no time for her to be married to you. You'll just have to take it back if you've asked her already."

"I've not asked her yet, but I'm going to today. She'll say yes because she loves me. She doesn't even like you, so it's doubtful if you asked her nicely to be your mistress, she'd agree." He said he had a good job and was considered a good catch. "You had a job. The board of Education fired you the day you were arrested. They've also done an extensive background check on you and found that you'd hurt women before."

"That's all water under the bridge. She wanted some time off to get married, and I didn't have a sub lined up to take her place. She argued with me, and I can't stand that." He asked why he'd not had anyone there for her. "Not that it's any of your business, but I forgot about it. She didn't need to get married anyway. She was a good teacher, and we all know what would have happened had she gotten married. She would have wanted time off to have a baby, and that would have been something else that I would have had to do. No, she was better off not getting married."

"She did get married and has two wonderful kids. Last I heard, she was no longer teaching but talking to others who had been abused by their bosses. That would be about you in the event that you didn't get that." He waved him off and asked about his job. "You've been fired and will no longer be able to have any sort of teaching position at any school so long as you live. You might say that you've been blackmarked against."

"What does Elaine get out of this? Hopefully, she got herself blackmarked, too." He told him what was going on with her job. "That's not fair. How does she get to keep her job?" He thought about that for a moment. "I suppose that it doesn't matter as she's going to be my mistress anyway. Having her work would be something that I'd have to keep an eye on her all the time. That's not going to work when I'm paying for everything."

"You have a real hard on for her being your mistress, don't you? Why? It's doubtful that you'd be able to survive when she was pissed off at you. Which would be all the time if you pull that crap on her like beating her up again." He said that she'd learn. "Doubtful. The only person that would have to learn would be you, and it's doubtful that you'd learn all that much when she starts laying down the law."

"We'll see." He told him it was all water under the bridge anyway, as she wasn't going to be his mistress. "Again, we'll see. I know what women like her need. I suppose you've been pampering her with her every whim. I'm not going to be doing that, so she might as well get that thought right out of her head."

"Like I said, the only person that would learn anything by this supposed relationship that you've made up in your mind is you." Erickson stood up, and so did he. "I only came here to tell you that she's going to be my wife soon, and for you to back off. Not that I think you'll be getting out of jail in the near future."

After he left him, taking his chair with him, he thought about what he'd said. Not getting out of jail soon was something that bothered him. How was that possible? He'd done nothing wrong that would warrant him being in trouble. Like he'd been thinking all along, she'd beaten him up as much as he'd done her. However, she was free to go about her business like nothing had happened to him.

Then there was the fact that he thought that he was going to marry her. That wasn't right, as he'd wanted her to be his mistress all along. Since she'd first come into his office. He knew now that he should have made his intentions clear then, but then she might not have taken the job. Some women didn't want to be reminded that they needed a man to take care of them all the time. He'd have to think on that some more to get it in his head how to best figure out how to make sure she understood that he'd been there for her first. Damn it all to heck and back, this wasn't fair, and he didn't like it.

~*~

Elaine was getting around well now. Walking the hallways, she could get about halfway around before she had to turn and walk back. She'd forgotten about that on the first day; that however far she walked, she was going to have to walk back to her room too. She'd had to have them take her back in a wheelchair because she'd been so shaky that she knew that she'd fall if she had to go back the way that she'd come.

She could see now, too. Not all that much, but enough to know that she was walking on a tile floor that was green and white and that the halls were the same color. Seeing Knox was a real treat as well since she'd been missing him so much when he'd been gone. Today, he had gone to see David, and she wondered how that had gone.

He was going to tell him that they were getting married. He'd never asked her if she'd marry him, but if he had, she'd say yes. They'd become very knowledgeable about one another, and she loved it when he told her stories of Martha. She sounded like the type of person that she would have liked and more than likely loved as much as she had her own mom. Her mom had passed away when she was thirteen.

While she'd never known her father when she was growing up, they'd never married, she did go and live with him when she'd been orphaned so young. He'd treated her well, but they never really had a good relationship like she did with her mom, and that had been all right too. She left home when she was eighteen and had never contacted him again. For all she knew, he could be dead now.

Knox was in her room when she got back from her evening walk. "I didn't think you'd be back so soon." He told her things hadn't gone well with David. "I'm sorry, but I did warn you. He's not a nice person to have to deal with. I know that firsthand."

"You do." He kissed her on her mouth, which was healing more daily. "He wants you as his mistress and is upset that you're getting married. Speaking of which." He got down on one knee, and she wanted to cry tears of happiness. "Will you do me the honor of being my wife forever? Will you allow me to pamper you and be pampered by you when I need it? Have children with me? Raise them to be good men and women? Will you please marry me so that I can feel whole?"

"Yes." He slipped the ring on her finger and kissed her hand. She could see that it was bright, but not too much more than that. "You'll have to tell me what it looks like. I can't see it through all my tears."

"It's a white diamond surrounded by smaller diamonds. It's a wide band, as I'm sure you can feel. Martha gave it to me when she passed away. I only saw her wear it on special occasions, but when she did, it made her shine with happiness. I think perhaps she bought it for herself so that she'd have something pretty to wear when she went out. I know that she wore it to my graduation when I got out of college." She kissed him, careful of her still-healing lips. The swelling was going down on them as well, but they were still cut up. It would be three weeks or more before she was able to get the stitches out. "I think it makes you shine more than it did her."

"Thank you so much." She asked about David. "How does he think it's going to work with us being married soon if I'm to be his mistress? I'm assuming that he has a plan."

"I think he just likes the way the word mistress rolls off his tongue. He has it in his head that you're going to be waiting on him to come to you with bated breath. And if you get out of hand, you can't hit him back, but he can pop you in the mouth was his exact words. He forgot that you were trained in combat duty when you were in the service and thinks that you fight unfairly. I nearly burst out laughing at that." She asked about his plans for a job and how he was going to pay for a mistress. "I think he believes he'll be able to con his way back into his job. He also thinks it's unfair that you didn't get put in jail for knocking him around."

"He's an idiot." Knox agreed with her. "I'm sure that he thinks that his wife is going to be all right with him having a mistress too." Knox told her how she'd left them. "Then I'd not be a mistress if he's not married. See? He's an idiot. I wonder where he got it into his head that I'd be okay with being his mistress? Surely not from anything that I said during my interview."

"Who knows how his mind works. I told him how he was going to be spending a lot of jail time, and he didn't seem to get that. Zander said that he'd sue him for attempted murder if nothing else. The fact that you fought back will have no bearing on the court proceedings at all." She asked about her being in the hospital and how that had any bearing on his getting put in prison. "It will play a big part in it. You've been hospitalized for three weeks now, and it looks like it might be a couple of more. A month in the hospital because you wouldn't be his mistress is a goodly amount of time for any reason."

The two of them talked about what kind of wedding she wanted, and she told him that the courthouse was fine by her. She didn't need nor want a big fancy wedding when going to the courthouse would do the same thing. He asked her if she'd miss it later.

"No. I mean, my parents had a big wedding, I've seen the pictures, and their marriage didn't work out. I'm not saying that ours won't work out, but why go to all that bother when we can just say our 'I do' at the courthouse and get to live the rest of our lives with each other. We can save our money and go on a huge honeymoon with the money we'll save."

"What an excellent idea. Where would you like to go? When you heal up, that is." She said she'd been all over the world, so seeing the States would be fine with her. "I like that idea. We can travel around, seeing what the country has to offer, and still save money. I know. Let's get us a camper and see the country that way. It would be fun to see the sights by driving to them, I think. That way, we can still save money. Though we really don't have to. We can do whatever we want and still not run out of money, love."

"I know, but this way we can take our time too. We won't have to be on a work schedule or anything. Just come and go as we please. Even if you have to work on some things for the family or with Zander, there's still the internet that you can send things back and forth with." He told her that he had not thought of that. "I think this is an excellent idea that you had. By the way, the doctor said that I can go home on Monday if I keep progressing the way that I am. Since this is Thursday, that gives me four days of working on getting out more and seeing around the hospital wing."

"That's wonderful news. Are you sure you don't mind me having dinner with my brothers tonight? I can cancel, no problem. We do this every Thursday night, and the women go out to dinner too." She said she wouldn't hear of him canceling out on a tradition that they have going on. "There won't be anyone around to sit with you. I'll be with the rest of them."

"I'll be fine. I'm getting around more and getting better at knowing when I've had enough. I'm going to be just fine, I know it. Besides, there is no reason for you to sit around here with me when you could be having fun with your brothers. I'm sure that you guys have a lot to say to one another." He said they end up staying late because of that. "Good. Then it's settled. You'll go to dinner with them and hear more gossip that you can come back and tell me about it. It's a win-win for the two of us. Besides, I don't want them to be mad at me because I had to have you miss the first dinner in a long time. Just go and have fun, and I'll be here when you're finished."

Her lunch was brought to her. It was still soft food, but it wasn't just mushy food. She had things like soup and rolls. They brought her ice cream as well as a shake that she could get some calories from. She wanted a burger and fries, but she'd have to wait a few more days for that. Her lips were still stitched up and sore.

"I have an idea that you'll love the house. I've been putting things away since I knew you were going to be living with me. I've been neglecting things by not putting them away. The library is now fully finished, being filled out." She asked him what he meant. "Since I moved in, the books have been in boxes. I just never got around to putting them away. A few other things too. I have a dining room with a table and chairs, but the chairs were still wrapped up from being moved in. It's not that I've been lazy, but I've never had anyone over who cared, so I didn't bother with getting things finished up. The kitchen is the only place that's been finished. And I think that solely on the cook. She wanted the space finished, and she did it on her own." They both laughed.

"I have my new apartment and all the new things that I have in it, as you know. I don't know what to do with all of that." He said she could sublet it out, and that way she'd not have to worry about it. Or he could buy out her lease, and she'd be finished. "I'll have to think about that. I've not paid any bills since I've been in here. I wonder how late my rent is now."

"I'll take care of it for you. I'll go by the realtor's office tomorrow and see what I can find out. I think that your utilities are all paid with your rent, so you don't have to worry about that." She asked him if he owned the apartment building. "I do. That and the houses on either side of it. I rent them out for the extra income."

"I wish I'd been that smart with my money. I was making good money when I worked overseas. But with the mess up of my checks, I was barely making it on my own without them." He said that she'd gotten it taken care of now. "Thanks to Shipley. I don't know how she did it, but she got the vice-president involved in my issues. I got my checks the next day."

"She's friends with both of them, the president as well. When she met Dusty, they gave her the paperwork that she needed to get out with full benefits. I know that she's still in contact with them, but what she does is anyone's guess." Elaine said that Shipley told her that she still has a house in DC that she uses when she has to go there. "Yes, I've stayed there as well when I had to do some work in the area. It's a huge house with lots of staff all the time. The government even rents it from her and keeps it safe when they have visitors who come to the White House. It's a nice setup for the two of them."

They talked about getting a camper, and since Knox had his laptop with him, they were able to look at the different kinds. They had thought about getting one they could drive everywhere they wanted to go, but then they'd have no car. They thought getting one that they pulled would serve them the best, and were excited about getting one for their trip.

"There's even a big barn on the property that I had built when I moved in. I didn't think of a camper being put in it, but I thought that lawn equipment would be stored in it for sure. It's a nice way to have them keep in good working order while they're not in use. There's plenty of room for a big camper." She asked how big he was talking. "As big as we can get. If we're going to be traveling in it all the time, we will need plenty of room. And when the kids come along, we'll take them with us as well. We'll make it a family thing."

"I love that idea." She did too. To travel with the kids to places that they could enjoy. "Now all I can think about is traveling around the country and having a good time. It'll have to wait until next year. I should be completely healed by then." He said that was the plan, but that didn't mean they couldn't take shorter trips to make sure they know what they're doing. "Good. Something like that could take a couple of trips to figure it out, I'm betting. Like, how do you even hook it up to a truck? I've seen them hooked up, but never how they do it."

"We'll figure it out. I'll hire someone to show us the ropes before we even leave the driveway." Elaine thought that was a wonderful idea. "Good. Then it's settled. We'll get us a camper and see what this old country has to offer us. We might want to watch some of the camping tips they have on the internet, too. Just so we can be prepared."

She thought that they could be prepared for anything, but still have trouble once they were out and about. There was no way that they could prepare for every little thing that came along. She was about as excited as she'd ever been for anything and couldn't wait until next summer.

Chapter 8

The courtroom was packed. David wondered if the people in this town had anything to do other than go to courtrooms when there was something going on. While he did work in the little burg, he didn't spend much time there. He liked it that way, and so had his family. He was going to have to ask someone how he was supposed to get in touch with his wife now that she'd run off with his kids.

He couldn't care less about the kids. They didn't do anything with him. Of course, they knew better than to ask him to play ball with them or something like that. He was a working man and the breadwinner. If they wanted to play, then they needed to do it with their mother. She didn't do anything all day long. It was her job to make sure they didn't bother him when he got home, either. He'd worked all day.

David had a plan. He was going to appeal to the judge's masculine side. Tell him how he'd never had a mistress before, and when he'd found one, she turned him down, and that's where the fight had come from. He was also going to talk to him about making Elaine become his mistress and have his wife come back home so that it would work for him. They were just being stubborn, and that wasn't fair to him. He'd worked hard on his appeal to the man he was going to be—

"This can't be right." He looked at the name placard on the big desk and was dismayed to find that it said Nora. Nora wasn't a man's name, and he didn't think that a woman would be able to hear his plea and give him what he wanted. And he wanted things to be the way they were about his job, too. There was no point in a woman—a woman could be for a woman, but a man had to be the judge for a man. That's the only way things would work out for him. As soon as they were told to all rise, he got his first look at Nora, the judge. She was definitely a woman. He raised his hand when she was seated. She asked him what he wanted. "Is there a man who can do your job for you today? I mean, I'm betting you're nice and all, but I have my notes all figured out for a man judge. Can't you just trade with someone? I had it figured that you'd be a man and would be more sympathetic toward me."

"What makes you think a man would be any more sympathetic than I would be?" He pointed out that she was a woman. "Women can be sympathetic towards men. Unless you're going to be spouting off things that not even a male judge would get behind. You're not going to be doing that in my courtroom today, are you?"

"I wanted a man because he might be all right with me having a mistress. And that won't work because you'd think I was wrong about wanting that." She told him she couldn't care less what he had in the way of extramarital affairs so long as his wife knew about it too. "You see, that's the problem. My wife left me when I got into trouble at school. In order for me to have a mistress, I have to have a wife."

"Usually that's the way it works out." He told her how he wanted her to make his wife come back to him so that his plans would work out. "You want to have a mistress, then just find someone willing to do that for you. You can call her whatever you want. You don't need a wife to have an affair."

"I really want her to be my mistress. And that's another thing. The woman that I have in mind doesn't want anything to do with me. She's actually marrying someone else so that she doesn't have to be my mistress. Now, is that fair?" Nora, the judge told him, she would have to be willing to be his whatever. "I don't think she's going to be willing unless you make her. See, a man would understand that and make Elaine, the woman that I want to be my mistress, he would make her be my mistress and make my wife come back so that it works out for me. She's the one who got me put in jail, too, my soon-to-be mistress, not my wife.

I knocked her around a bit, but she did the same back to me. That's not fair either that she got to stay in the hospital and I had to stay in jail."

"That's why you're really here, isn't it? You beat up an innocent woman in the parking lot of the school because she didn't want to be your mistress, correct?" He said that he'd tried reasoning with her, but she wouldn't have it. "Then I'm afraid that I can't help you. I told you that in order for you to have a mistress, she had to be willing. It sounds to me like you'd be better off finding yourself someone else rather than this Elaine person."

"But I want her. You see, you're not helping me at all. A man would help me out in this. You can see her right over there. She's the one who looks like she'd been beaten up." Nora, the judge asked how Elaine was doing. When she said she'd been better, he rolled his eyes. What did her health have to do with anything that was going on in this courtroom? He raised his hand again to be heard. "Are you going to make her or be nice to her? I tried that, and she wouldn't have it. In fact, while I was trying to get things set up for her to be my mistress, she went out to dinner with a man. I'm thinking that one right here by her."

"I know who they are, Mr. Sheen. I married the two of them not an hour ago. They had all the right paperwork and witnesses to make it work for them."

He said she wasn't being fair. "Fair or not, she's not going to be your mistress when she's just married Mr. Knox Erickson. At this point, the only thing she could be to you is an affair, but I doubt very much that's going to happen either. They're well and truly in love with each other, and that's about it for you."

"Things are not going the way that I want them to, and that's not right. I had plans, you see, and she's messing them up by being married. Can't you void their marriage for me? A man would do it. I know that he would." Nora, the judge told him, it was doubtful that anyone would void their marriage as they looked to be in love. "I don't care who she's in love with. I wanted her to be my mistress first, and he didn't have any right to marry my girl."

"Mr. Sheen. Why don't we get down to why you're really here? You beat Mrs. Erickson nearly to death that morning, then left her in the cold to die. You've already admitted that you did it because she wouldn't be your mistress. Is that the way you settle things by bringing a ball bat to convince someone to do what you want? You've done this sort of thing before." He said that was different; she'd been wanting time off. "And you couldn't see it in your schedule to allow her to be off for her wedding? That's not right either."

"I forgot to find someone who would cover for her, and she got pissy with me. She's a good teacher, and I didn't want to have to work all that hard to get someone to come in and mess up her room and kids for her. If you think of it that way, I was doing her a favor by not allowing her the time off to get married so that things would be perfect the way that they were. She never did thank me for that either." Nora, the judge asked him why he'd beaten either woman up when they worked for him. "That's it right there. They worked for me, and I was their boss. They should have known better than to disobey me when I'd told them how things were going to go. No one has any respect for the working man anymore. You have to make Elaine mine so that I can have a mistress."

"I think you just like the sound of that name you've come up with." He said it was sexy sounding. "Sexy or not, it's not going to happen. You've beaten a woman nearly to death twice for not getting your way, and I'm going to remand you over for trial for next year. About September should give you plenty enough time to see that your way isn't always the right way."

"Will you make my wife come back to me? That's the least you can do since you took away my mistress from me." Nora, the judge told him that she thought that his wife was better off without him around. "Well, that's just not right. I need her around so that someone cleans my other house. I don't know what she does all day while I'm working, but I know that I like having dinner on the table when I get home."

"Well, aren't you just the modern man?" David smiled at her. It was the first thing that she had said to him all morning that was nice. "You'll spend your time awaiting trial in the local jail. Also, while we're talking about the local jail, you'll not have contact with either your wife or Mrs. Erickson while you're awaiting trial. Do you understand me?"

"Then how am I supposed to convince her that I'm the man for her. Elaine is just playing hardball, and I don't like it. You should tell her that she has to come and visit me daily so that I can let her see what she's missing." Nora, the judge said no. Just like that, just no, like that was final. "You have to give me something. I'm going to be locked in the local jail for nearly a year, and in all that time, I'm supposed to just wait? What am I supposed to do? Who do I get to talk to? The police aren't very nice to me since they know I beat up Elaine."

"They're not your friends, and I applaud them for treating you like an inmate. You can talk to yourself for all I care, just leave the women alone." Nora, the judge looked at him. "For that matter, you're to leave anyone alone who tells you that they don't want anything to do with you. Understand me? When they tell you 'no', then you're to leave them alone too. Not having the police call them for you either."

"Well, it's going to be a boring year for me. Can I at least have me some pens and paper? I have to make notes on things I'm going to do when I get out of jail." Nora said that he could have one sheet of paper at a time and one pencil. Nothing more. "Not even a magazine or two? How about me getting a television I can keep up with my shows on? This ain't fair, you know. She beat me up too and gets to be out doing things like she wants to do."

"She was defending herself against you. There is a difference. She wouldn't have been beating on you at all had you left your ball bat at home and not touched the poor woman. Now, as for your other requests, I'm going to leave that up to the police captain. He'll know what you need and what you don't." She banged the gavel on the desk and then pointed at him. "You'll behave while in jail, or I'll send you right to prison on the next trip, see that I don't."

He tried to get someone to answer him about his television while they were taking him back to his cell. David didn't understand why it was such a big deal. He'd made promises that he'd not have it on all night. Unless there was something that he wanted to watch. And he said that he'd turn it down when there were others around, but if they went to sleep, then he'd turn it back up. They didn't listen to him as usual, and he was getting kind of pissed about it. Someone had to want him to be happy when he wasn't allowed to talk to anyone for a whole year.

By then, Elaine might even have a baby. That would just ruin everything. Her body would be all stretched out like she'd carried around fifty pounds of fat, then lost it. He knew what a body would look like after giving birth; his own wife had done it to herself when she'd gotten pregnant with their kids. And he wasn't allowed to tell her not to get in the family way because he wasn't allowed to talk to her. Things were being messed with that he didn't care for.

When they were taking him back to his cell, he asked for his pencil and paper. They said they'd get it when they had time. Well, he wanted to start on his list now, not when they had time. He had several things already that he wanted to put on one sheet of paper that would about fill it up. David was going to have to write really small, so he'd have everything on his list that he had, so as not to forget them. His mind was too willy for him at the moment, and he couldn't think straight. He was blaming that on Elaine right away. If she'd just done what he wanted, then things would have been better off for him.

Sitting on the edge of his cot, he put his head between his legs and sat there. It had worked when he'd been a boy to calm his mind down. It only happened when he was thinking too hard, and sometimes at work, he'd have to do this when the teachers were going on about something that they wanted. Usually wanting more things for their rooms, but he had to deal with it the only way he knew how. And that was to do what he was doing now. Shut the world out and calm his breathing down enough where he could count them. Sitting up, when someone said his name, they asked him if he was all right.

"I will be. Got me some breathing issues when I get excited." The officer asked him what he had to be excited about. "My list. When I make one up, I get too excited and have to breathe this way to get my mind to relax. I'm all right now. Just have a bit of a headache."

"You want to see the doctor?" He said that he would like something for his headache, but no, he didn't want to see a doctor. "I can't give you nothing without his approval. I'll have to call the doc in to have him say it's okay to give you something, even if it's just an antacid. I'll give her a call and see—"

"Is that all that works around here is women? Gees Louise. Would it be too much to ask if the chief of police is a man, then? Someone who would know what it's like to be a man who isn't allowed to talk to anyone?" David was told that the chief was a man and that the doc was also their corner. "Great. So long as she realizes that I'm a living man, not a dead one, I guess that will be all right."

The doc was called, and he was allowed something for his head. But she was going to examine him first thing in the morning. David couldn't win today, and he wasn't happy that he wasn't going to get a television to watch. The chief had said no, and that was final. Everything against him was final, and he didn't much care for it either.

~*~

Elaine got her stitches out of her lips this morning, and she was feeling good about herself. Not only was she getting around better, but she could walk all the way to the mailbox and back without any trouble now. She was able to do things that she'd not been able to do in the six weeks since she'd been hurt, like washing all of her hair instead of just the ends because of the wounds.

"You look like you feel better, too." She told Shipley that she did, and it felt wonderful to feel good. "I'm glad you do. I might have you sign on as my assistant in the office I now hold. What do you think about being a medical examiner's assistant?"

"I could do that for you. It sounds like something that I did when I was out of the country. I only did it a couple of times, but it wasn't that bad." She said she'd been using Locke, but since he's so busy with his patients at the hospital, it was getting harder for him to help her. "I think that would be just the job that I've been looking for. It'll get me out of the house for sure."

"That's the reason that I do it. And because of the people waiting for death certificates. There was quite a backlog when I first started. I'm only just now getting things caught up there. It wouldn't be something that we do daily, I hope not anyway, but so far it's only been about two a month. Mostly from the nursing home." She asked what she had to do. "Nothing more than you did when you were a nurse. Just assist me with the post-mortems and help me keep up with paperwork, too. We can do a couple if you want to wait and decide if you want to do it or not. I'm easy."

"I think that it would be a good job. I'm not so sure about going back to class and teaching. I drove by the parking lot the other day and had to pull over. It made me so upset. I might not be able to teach again, but this I think I could do." Shipley said today she was working for the police department as a doctor for one of the inmates. "It's probably David. I think that he was the only one who stayed in jail when they were all sent off to prison. I don't want anything to do with him."

"I don't either now that you mention it. But I'll go and examine him today because I said that I would." Elaine asked if she had to do that often. "No. He's going to be there for a year, so at some point, he might get hurt, and I have to go and attend to him. So if I have something to work with at the beginning, I'm not going to be blind sided by him when something goes wrong. He's a dick weed, I heard."

"He's a prick, is what he is." The two of them laughed. "He really wasn't that bad when I first met him. Sometime between him interviewing me and Knox and me going out a few days later, he got it into his head that I was going to be his mistress. As Knox said when he talked to him, it was like he heard the word and liked it, so he used it until he figured out what it meant. Like I said, I want nothing to do with him or his illnesses. It wouldn't matter to me if he were to get some incurable disease and fade out of my life."

"You don't mean that." She said that she didn't, but didn't want to have to deal with him anymore. "I can understand that. You've only just gotten your feet under you again, and you don't want to go with me to examine him. It would be nice, but I understand. Maybe Locke can spare a nurse to get blood for me while I'm there. That would keep me from having to stick him several times to draw it."

Shipley made a call, and not only could Locke spare a nurse, but he sent over the equipment for her to get tissue samples, too, if she needed them. David would be taken to the hospital in a couple of days to get a full body workup to make sure that his stay with the police was going to be a healthy one. He would be put on a special diet too, so that he remained in good shape for when he went to prison, if that was a possibility after his trial date.

Elaine was excited about her new job. She'd been having nightmares about going back to the school to teach. She had loved her job, but David had ruined it for her. He'd ruined a great many things for her, and one of them was her relationship with Knox. She had a feeling by now they'd be sleeping together, and because of David beating her nearly to death, she'd had to wait until her stitches were out so that she could make love with him.

That was her plan, too. If she were honest with herself, she was sort of afraid to have sex with Knox. Not scared but nervous. She knew that her skin was still beaten up in places, and she had fresh scars all over her back and legs. The ones that were on her lips had healed nicely, but she could still see the scars from the stitches that she'd had in them.

Her eyes were no longer swollen shut, but she had two black eyes that made her look terrible in the mirror. Her left ear was tender to the touch, and she had to be careful when she brushed her teeth, or they would bleed because of the cuts that she had on her gums. In a word, she was a mess. It made her cry whenever she looked in the mirror because of what David had done to her.

"What's going on?" She turned and looked at Knox when he stood in front of the bathroom door where she was examining herself. "You look beautiful without the stitches in your mouth. How did it go?"

"It went well. He said I had to keep sunscreen on so that they don't discolor when I get too much sun on them. But otherwise, I'm just fine." She tried to turn away from him, but he wasn't having it. "I have a job working with Shipley as a post-mortem assistant. I won't have to go on jail runs with her if they involve David, but she is getting a nurse from the hospital to help her out with those."

"Look at me." She smiled and turned to look at him, but her eyes were heavy with her unshed tears. "Oh, baby, don't cry. David won't be able to hurt you anymore. If he gets out in a year, which I don't see happening, I told you that Zander is going for the maximum, then we'll deal with him then. In the meantime, he's in jail and no longer a problem for you and me."

"It's not all, David. I'm so ugly. How can you stand to look at me?" He pulled her into his arms and held her while she sobbed against his chest. "I hate what I look like, and I was hoping we could have sex when I got the stitches out of my mouth. Now look at me. I'm ugly with all these scars and scabs all over my body. I found one on my hip that I'd not known about until I was pulling on my pants this morning. Will it be like this all the time? Where I'm suddenly finding another place that he knocked me around with?"

He held her tightly, and she loved him for that. When she mentioned her hip again, he sort of laughed a bit. Looking up at him, she asked him what he found so funny, ready to do battle if he made fun of her. He only shook his head and then leaned his forehead onto hers.

"I love you so much. And I would love it if we were to have sex tonight. But no pressure. I don't even see the scars or scabs anymore. I only see how beautiful you are and how brave you are." She said she didn't feel beautiful at all. Then she pointed out her black eyes as well as the scarring on her head and arms. "All things that make me realize how brave you were when you were being hurt. I believe that other women would have given up and let him beat them. But not you. He's going to have his scars and scabs for the rest of his life. Perhaps not the scabs, but the scars for sure. You'll do what's right with them, and they'll be nothing but a faint memory someday that will fade with them."

"But I want to have sex with you." He threw back his head and laughed. "I don't think this is the least bit funny, you know. I have been thinking about making love with you since we started living together. And today, when the stitches were taken out of my mouth, I thought it would come true, but then I remembered what I look like."

"I see you beyond the black eyes. And they'll heal. Sometime in the near future, they'll be as faded away as the other wounds that he put on your body." She asked him how much longer. "It doesn't matter. Not to me. I have you, and he doesn't. I feel like I've won the best prize of all the things that I could have gotten by having you in my life."

"You're being too nice to me." He told her that he needed to be laid. "I see how you are. You just want to have sex with me and will butter me up to have it. Is that right?"

"No. I want to make love to you because I love you so very much." He couldn't have said anything more romantic than that, and the timing was perfect. "I couldn't care less what you have on your face or eyes. I love a part of you that is perfect. You're heart."

"You're the best thing that has ever happened to me." He told her that he felt the same way about her. "I'd love to have you make love with me. I have been thinking of nothing else since I got back from the doctor's office. Of course, I'd not looked in the mirror until I got back, but I'm sure you can close your eyes while we do it."

"I want to see every part of you when I make love with you. I want to see the passion in your eyes. The way your breathing stops when you're about to come. I want to taste you when you come too." She felt her face heat up a little at what he was saying to her. "There are so many things that I want to do with your body that I'm afraid that one time won't be enough. We'll have to make love for months so that I can taste you everywhere I wish."

"You're making me wet." He said good, and smiled at her. However, the look in his eyes had her seeing lust there, and she knew she felt the same way. "How about we have some dinner and then go up to the bedroom? I think that would be the perfect place to start our new relationship."

"I love the way that you think." He kissed her again, and she could feel his erection at her abdomen. Moving against him, she felt his body shudder, and she wanted more. Reaching down between them, she cupped his cock in her hand. "You keep that up, and we'll never have dinner, much less make it up to the bedroom. I want you now and later, love. How about we skip dinner and have each other for our meal. I think that sounds so much better, don't you?" She whimpered a bit and told him she loved the way that he thought. "I love you so very much, Elaine Erickson. And will for the rest of my days."

"And I love you too, Knox Erickson, and am so happy that you found me when you did. Who knew that moving into an apartment could get me someone to love with all that I am. And to have you love me back was more than I could have ever dreamed of." They kissed again, and he pulled away. She could see his erection now and was glad that he was holding her. "I want you. Now."

He picked her up in his arms, and she laughed. As they headed to the bedroom, he told her all the things he was going to do to her. First of all, she was to take every bit of her clothing off and have a look at the treasures that she'd been keeping from him. She couldn't wait.

Chapter 9

Knox felt his frustrations when he tried to open the first button on her blouse. But when he looked at her, he could see a part of her that he'd never seen before. Trust. It made a calm roll over him in such a way that he knew he'd be able to do this without hurting her. The rest of the buttons seemed to open themselves for him, and he pulled it off of her and dropped it to the floor.

"I've never been undressed before." Knox told her that he'd never undressed anyone before. "Good. I like knowing that I'm first for something. You must have a lot of experience with making love to women."

"You're the only one that counts." He kissed her again, gently prying her mouth open so that he could taste what she had there. "You taste like mint and a sweetness that I've never tasted before."

"Mint chocolate chip. I treated myself at the Dairy Mart when I got the stitches taken out. It's my favorite ice cream." He reached behind her and tried to undo her bra. "It's in the front of my bra. See? It's got these really nice hooks that don't dig into me."

"I've got it now." He slowly undid the hooks

that held her breasts from him. While he didn't remove her bra, he could see the curves of them as they were hidden from him. Unsnapping her pants, he had her sit on the side of the bed so that he could remove them. Standing her up again after getting her jeans off, she stood before him in just her bra and panties. It was nearly too much for his body to see what he'd never been able to have before. "You're more beautiful than I ever imagined."

"My turn." He didn't want her to strip him down, but he stood still while she undid his tie. He'd been at work earlier and had already removed his jacket when he got home. After getting his shirt off and his cuff links undone, he watched as she walked to the dresser and laid them onto the tray that was there. He nearly bit his tongue when she walked toward the dresser. Her body seemed to shimmer in the evening light.

When she took his shirt off, she ran her fingers from his wrist to his shoulders to the back of his neck and down the other arm. He felt his cock leak and knew that he was going to come soon if she kept up with what she was doing. When she leaned in and licked his nipple, he had to adjust himself twice so that he wouldn't hurt. As soon as she took his belt off, he knew that he wasn't going to make it if she kept this up. When she undid his pants and pulled the zipper down, he had to sit down on the side of the bed or pass out. She was making love to him, and he wasn't even naked. He loved every second of it.

When she removed his pants with his briefs, he had to lean back on the bed or pass out. The cool breeze in the room had his cock aching, and he whimpered when she touched her finger to his crown. There was nothing he could do but allow her to do whatever she wanted to him until he was finished. And he figured that it was going to be in the next ten seconds if she kept up what she was doing to him.

Sitting across his lap, he leaned up and removed her bra. Her panties had to go next, and since they were nothing more than a couple of patches of silk and some strings, he pulled them off with a single yank of his hands. She must have come a little because she cried out his name. He felt like the king of the world as she looked down at him from her perch on his lap.

"I want to fuck you like this." He nearly came again, his eyes rolling to the back of his head. "I want to ride you like this so that I can come all over you."

"I'm not going to be able to last." She smiled at him, a devilish sort of smile that made his heart skip a few beats. "I want you to do whatever you want to me, then I'm going to do the same to you."

"Promise?" He nodded, and when she sat up, he held his cock while she lowered herself down over him in small movements that had his heart beating hard in his chest. When she was seated as deeply as he could manage, he moved upward and deepened his cock inside of her. "You feel so good right here. I love the way that you fill me."

"Ride me, love." She did, her movements off a little, but once she got the rhythm of movements down, she had him lie back on the bed so that she had full access to him. The first thing she did was pinch his nipples until they ached. He wanted to taste her, but she was enjoying herself so much that it was all he could do not to roll her to her back and take her hard.

When she leaned down and took his nipple in her mouth again, he wrapped his hands around her ass and pulled her down so that he could go deeper inside of her. Kissing him, making her way up from his nipple to his mouth, he took her mouth hard as he fucked her. Rolling her to her back, he was as deep as he could go when she wrapped her legs around his hips. Fucking her with his hands still at her ass, he took her as hard as he could, mindful of her wounds as he did so. Christ, she was more than he'd ever dreamed of her being, and he wanted her all.

Lifting her breast up so that he could suckle at her nipple, he felt her come when she tightened around his shaft. When she came a second, then a third time, it was all he could do to hold onto her while she shivered and shuddered beneath him. Digging her nails in his back nearly sent him over the edge, but he knew that there was going to be something epic coming to the two of them, and he couldn't wait. Taking as much of her breast into his mouth as he could, he bit down hard to have her crying out again.

His body was primed for his release. He could feel it coming from the bottom of his feet to his cock and then to his head as he fucked her harder still. When she stiffened beneath him, he watched her face until she screamed. That was all it took for him to fall over the edge with her and pass out.

He couldn't have been out for more than a few seconds, but it was enough for him to know that nothing had changed. She was still beneath him, and his cock was still hard for her. As he moved in and out of her, she cried out again, and he smiled. Even unconscious like she was, he could still bring her to a peak. She looked up at him as he held her.

"That was better than I ever thought it would be, and I had some pretty high expectations." He laughed; he couldn't help himself. Glad that she was all right, he kissed her gently on the mouth and rolled to his back, taking her with him as he did so. "I could sleep for a week, I think." He moved inside of her. "Or not. Are you ready for another round?"

"I don't know. I just love holding you like this."

He didn't move all that much more because his body was spent. "I think I could join you in that sleep. I feel like I'd get a good night's sleep for the first time in years."

They dozed off and on and made love when they woke. There wasn't another climax like they'd had, but they did enjoy themselves a great deal. When her belly growled for the third time, he thought that it was time that the two of them got up and found something to eat. It was well past midnight when they got out of bed and pulled on their pajamas, him the bottoms and her the top to them to go downstairs. He hoped there was something easy to eat in the refrigerator because he didn't have it in him to make something work for them. The ham that had been baked earlier in the day was the perfect thing for them to munch on. Slicing pieces of it off and simply eating it with cheese as their bread was fun as well as just what they wanted. Once they polished off as much as they wanted, he found some grapes in the crisper, and they fed them to each other while talking about how good they felt.

He did too. Like he'd been waiting for her to come along and love him so that he could feel the happiness that was there when you found the one true love of your life. And he felt that more and more daily that she'd been made just for him.

Going back up to bed, they made love slowly this

time. Touching one another like they were memorizing their skin. He knew every place on her that made her sigh and giggle. She was very ticklish, and he loved that. At one point, they both dozed off, and when he woke, the room was flooded with light.

Surprised that it was nearly eleven in the morning when he woke, he stayed in bed to watch Elaine sleep. She was beautiful despite the fact that she was still bruised up. There was blood on her lip, too, that he must have taken her mouth too hard at some point. Sorry for that, he decided that he was going to be more careful with her in the future and vowed to never hurt her again if he could help it. When she stretched and looked at him with a tired smile, she asked him why he was staring at her.

"I was thinking how absolutely beautiful you look." She snorted, and that caused him to laugh. "You're such a romantic. I wonder how I never noticed that before."

"You just want to get laid again. But to be honest, I think I'm a bit sore." He promised her that he was as well. "Then we need to get a hot shower together and start our day. What time is it anyway?"

After telling her the time, she nearly leapt from the bed. But when she sat back down, he told her to be careful as she made her way to the bathroom. He wouldn't admit this to anyone, but when he stood up to join her in the shower, he was dizzy too. They'd burned a great deal of calories last night, and he didn't know if he could make it without holding onto things as he went. As soon as he got into the shower with Elaine, he did feel better but not great. He was sore from the bottom of his feet to his head. Christ, who knew that having sex, especially as much as they'd had, could render a person weak as a newborn. And he'd do it all over again, too, if given the chance.

They didn't do anything but hang around the house. At some point, they ate lunch and enjoyed more of the ham, but other than that, they just hung out together and talked. It was a special day for the two of them, and he didn't want to ruin it by talking about David or any of the crap he'd pulled on her. One only had to look at Elaine to know what he'd done, but for the most part, they talked about the upcoming holidays and the plans they were going to make for next summer. The camper was going to be epic for them, and he couldn't wait to go shopping for one.

"I want one with more than one bedroom. So that we can have an office if we need it." He said that he liked that idea and would get him another laptop to leave in the thing while they were home, too. "You'll need to have it updated if you do that too much. I only know that because I heard someone saying something about it when I was working. Two of the teachers have campers that they use every weekend."

"I read that you should have a shakedown close to home the first few times so that you know if you needed something, you can run home and get it." Elaine said that she thought that they'd have so much fun no matter where they went. "I agree. This will be the perfect thing we can do with our free time, and since we both have jobs that don't require us to be at home all the time, we can take weeks off at a time to have a mini vacation."

"That would be good. Just come and go as we please." He was warming up to the idea and wished that they could have had this summer to have gone on some trips too. "We'll have to make sure that the house is safe as well. Like stopping our mail when we're gone."

"That would be easy enough. Or have one of my brothers pick it up for us. They'd do it no problem. Maybe they'll all get campers, and we can make a road trip of it. I think that they'd enjoy that as well." She looked so happy that he wanted to make this work for them right now. "I'll do some research on campers. That's what I do for Zander. I'll have just what we need when we're ready to buy, so that we get the best one we can. I'm excited for summer again, and it's not even Thanksgiving. What will we do when the snow is on the ground, and we can't travel?"

"Travel someplace warmer, I guess." He said that he could do that too. Though Tennessee didn't get all that cold in the winter months, they could still travel as far as they wanted. He wanted to see the country like they'd talked about before. "I'll have to get in better shape so that we can do some hiking."

"I run. I've not been doing it lately in favor of being with you, but I can get back in the habit soon." She said that she used to run as well and had run in marathons while out of the country. "I didn't know that. We'll have to do that as well if we can get into good enough shape."

They talked about getting into shape and decided that they'd need a gym membership or buy some kind of equipment for home. He was all for the gym; he did better about getting things done if he had to pay for it. She was of the same opinion; she did better when there were other people around to compete with. Something else that he didn't know about her was that she was competitive. He loved that about her, too.

~*~

Shipley ordered the usual tests on someone who was in the jail system so that he'd be able to say nothing about how they were treating him. David complained and bitched about everything that was being done to him, and she tried to ignore it. No wonder Elaine didn't want to be around him; he was a whiny baby about everything.

"How much blood do you need? It seems like you're draining me dry." She told him to shut up. "You don't have much of a bedside manner, do you. I thought you were supposed to be nice to your patients."

"You're not my patient, but a person that I'm making sure doesn't have any complaint to bitch about later down the line. You will be put on a diet plan too that's going to keep you healthy." He whined that he didn't need to be on a diet. "Well, that's too bad. What I say goes, and you're just lucky that I don't put you on a bland diet that has no taste whatsoever."

"You'd be mean like that. I want another doctor." She told him that she was it and that he was lucky that no one else was around to put up with his bullshit. "Well, the least you can do is be nice to me. I've had some pretty bad blows to my life of late. Did I tell you that I'm not allowed to talk to the two women in my life who were supposed to be there for me?"

"I know one of them. Elaine is my sister-in-law by marriage." He asked how she was doing without him around. "Better than you'll be doing if you don't shut up and listen to what I'm saying to you. I told you three times that you need to give me a urine sample."

"I don't have to pee all that much." She explained to him again how she didn't need all that much. "Well, if you're going to test it, there should be enough for me to give you something. I have just a little bit of dribble, and that's all." She wanted to slap the shit out of him again. It had been like this since she'd gotten him in a room at the hospital.

"Does your husband have a mistress?" Shipley told him no, that she was more than enough for him. "If you treat him like you are me, I'm betting that he'd jump at the chance to have one. You're kind of mean all the time."

"I have better things to do than to hang around you." He was quiet for about ten minutes. She'd bet anything that he was trying to figure out what she'd been saying to him. For someone who worked in a school system, he was fairly stupid. She wondered if they gave tests to be able to be around children and decided that he more than likely cheated. "I'm ready for that sample. Give it to me, or I'm going to squeeze it out of you by milking our penis."

"You can't do that." She told him to watch her. "Gees Lousie, you're mean. I bet if you had any kids, they'd be bullies."

"No, they wouldn't because I would never bully them. It's you I don't like, and that's why I'm treating you like I have been. You hurt someone that I love." He snorted at her and took the sample bottle with him to the bathroom. She wanted to give him instructions again, but it would be a waste of time. He seemed bent on doing things wrong for her. "Hurry up. I don't have all day to waste on your ass."

"I'm coming." She didn't find anything wrong with him so far, but there were test results that still had to come back. Most of them had already, and he was in good health. It was keeping him that way for the next year that bothered her. He didn't seem to understand that he had to eat better now that he was in the system. He handed her a nearly full cup of urine when he came out of the bathroom. "I had to strain that much out for you. I don't want to have to do that again, so make sure you do it right the first time."

She was going to kill him and save the state a great deal of money on a trial. As she dipped the stick in the urine, she waited for the result while thinking of the number of people who would thank her for killing him. He was nothing but a little shit anyway, so no one would miss him if he suddenly turned up missing. She'd bet that even the police would be thrilled that he was gone.

"Everything is good." He asked about the urine test and what it was for. "To check to see if you're diabetic or have any kind of infection. You don't. So I don't want to hear about you having issues as soon as you get back to jail."

"Why are you sending me back? Isn't there a room that I could be put in for the night? I'd love to be able to watch some television for a night." She told him no, he was going back to jail. "You're just mad about having to test me. That's all. I'm betting that when you get home, you're going to remember a test you didn't run, and I'm going to be right back here getting them done. Won't it save you time just to make sure by letting me stay the night so that in the event that you remember something, I'll be right here where I can have them ran?"

"No. I didn't forget anything because I have a list that I have to perform on you. I followed it and did whatever I was required to do." He looked like a child who had had his favorite toy taken from him. "Straighten up, jack ass, before I have to probe you."

He put his hands over his dick, and she laughed. It was the most fun she'd had all day with him, and she was glad that he understood that she'd do it too. As soon as he was chained back up, he asked about spending the night again, and she didn't bother answering him. She'd said no, and that was final. He hated it when she said that to him, she'd noticed and was glad that she'd been able to work it into a conversation with him. The man was an idiot, and she didn't like that the state was going to be taking care of him for the next year while he waited on his trial. He should have been sent to prison with the rest of the perverts, and that would have been the end of her contact with him. She didn't like him simply for the reason that he'd hurt Elaine. Shipley thought that was a good enough reason to hate anyone.

As she made her way home, she thought about the tests that she'd run, making sure that she didn't forget one. Not that she'd go back and redo it, but she didn't want to have to see him again. Not only was he whiny about things, she thought that he was a little shitter too.

Dusty was home when she got there, and she was glad to see him. When she explained what she'd been doing, he got a kick out of the fact that she'd had to yell at him several times about his attitude.

"He's worse than a little kid." He told her that he'd heard that about him from Elaine. "I don't know how she put up with him at the school when she was there. And with him wanting her to be his mistress, he must have been really bad."

"He didn't bring it up with her until the day he beat her up. She'd had no clue that he wanted anything like that from her." Shipley asked what he'd said to her about it. "Nothing much the day before. He just acted like he normally does when she was there. Friendly and talked to her a little too closely. But she just wrote that off as being like he was. It wasn't until he was beating her to shit that he made his intentions clear to her. At least that's what I heard from Knox."

"I guess he would know." Shipley kissed Dusty on the mouth and told him that she loved him. "I love you so much that I sometimes wonder if I'm going to bust with it."

"You are such a romantic." She snorted at him, and he laughed. "There's my girl. How about we get in touch with my brothers and see if they want to have dinner tonight? It's the cook's night off, so we'd have to go out anyway. It might be fun to get all together."

"I'd love that. Someplace with a buffet. I was hoping for something that I could get my fill with." He said that he knew of two places that she might like, and he let her pick while he contacted his family. "How about soon, too. I'm suddenly starving."

By the time he had contacted his family, she had showered and changed. She didn't want to smell like David did and was glad that she'd been able to wash some of him off her. Getting dressed in something casual, she was glad that the others were able to meet them there. She was going to have to get herself something small to eat, or she'd never make it. As she was making herself some cheese and crackers, Dusty joined her in the kitchen.

"They're all for it." Good, she told him that would be fun for them. "I've called ahead to the restaurant to let them know that there would be about fifteen people with the kids who would be coming in.

They said that they'd have us a room and would put in some extra platters for us when we arrived. I thought that was nice of them."

"I do too. We don't want to make it so that they'll go out of business because we decided to show up." He said that they could put a dent in some buffet stuff when they were all hungry. "All right. If you're ready to go, we can head there. Locke and Alex will be a little late, but they said to start without them. They're shopping for baby things and have to unload their car before they can go."

The drive was about twenty minutes, but it seemed longer. She really was hungry and wanted to eat sooner rather than later. Shipley knew that she shouldn't have skipped lunch while working, but she wanted to get the tests done and over with for David. He'd been too much of a pain in the ass for her to want to linger all that long waiting for the rest of the tests if she'd stopped long enough to eat. Her way, she was only gone an hour rather than the two that it would have normally taken her to get through them all.

She didn't even wait to sit down, but went right up to the buffet line to get something so she'd not be so starved. There was soup to be had, too, but she wanted something substantial in her belly, and soup wouldn't cut it. She was glad to see that two others from their party had joined her, and she wasn't the only one who was starving. There was a lot to be said for buffets, and getting food immediately was one of the best perks she could find.

After her second plate, she was able to slow down a bit. While still hungry, she wasn't as starved as she'd been. Tasting the food now rather than gulping it down, she was happy when the restaurant refilled most of the trays. She was getting her fourth plate of food when someone brought up Martha. She didn't mind them talking about her because she wished that she could have gotten to meet the woman. She did a lot for the men in her life, and she wanted to be able to thank her for it.

"She loved buffets. Though I don't know why, she rarely ate enough to feed a bird." Jack brought up the fact that they ate a lot and perhaps didn't notice when she refilled her plate. "That could be it. We could eat like we'd been starved whenever we came here. This was one of her favorite places to eat."

"Remember when she took us to that seafood place out on Vine? We never went back after they told us that we could only have one plate of food per person. Martha wrote a review about the place, and I think they went out of business the following year. I know it wasn't much too long after we'd been there."

"They'd been having trouble anyway." Shipley had heard that one scathing remark from Martha would shut a place down faster than the city could. She was glad that she'd had nothing to do with a place going under. "I think that's why they said we could only have the one plate. They were trying to keep people in the seats and save money on the food bill. That's a sad way to have a place that is supposed to be all you can eat."

They talked about the days that they'd had this week, and even she had something to comment on, too. The other women, especially Elaine, had plenty to say as well, and she was happy for it. It had been approved that she could hire her as an assistant, and Shipley was thrilled. It would make the work that she had to do less boring to her, and having a second set of hands would make things go faster, too. She wouldn't cut corners, not on something like that, but it would be nice to have someone to talk to when they were getting ready or finished up. She liked Elaine and was looking forward to working with her.

She loved working with the other women, too, but there was something so special about Elaine that she enjoyed her company, too. She was smart and funny, and she had a second sense about her that made Shipley think she'd be the perfect person to work with under stress. It could be stressful working as medical personnel, and she wanted someone there who would make it seem less stressful for the two of them. She knew that she had picked the perfect person for the job.

Chapter 10

Zander had the paperwork for his brothers in neat piles. The contracts for Locke were approved for him to sign them, and he had even made marks in places where he could see the loopholes that favored himself. There were no typos in the entirety of the contracts, which made him think that someone took their time with them and made sure they were right the first time they sent them over. Then there were the ones for his brother Demi.

They were so full of typos that he wondered if the person typing them had gotten out of grade school yet. They spelled the name of the company wrong on one of the contracts, not once or twice, but a total of seventeen times, and a different way each time. It was messily written, too. He wouldn't have signed them even if every loophole in them was a guarantee for them to win bushels of money. If a person didn't take their time on a contract that they wanted you to sign, then there was no point in doing business with them. They were going to be messy at it as well.

"I have an appointment at one o'clock today. Did you want to go with me?" He told Locke that he had the contract finished for his meeting and that he could sign it if he wanted. "That's good to know. They've been really wanting me to get it filed. I've been having second thoughts about it."

"Then don't do it." He asked him what he meant. "You've always trusted your gut. Don't not do that now. If it feels bad to you, then I'd not sign it, no matter what the contract says. I can tell them for you if you want. You know I have no trouble telling people no."

"Yes, and I love that about you." He sat down in the chair across from his desk. "I don't know what it is about the company that wants us to invest in it is about but I have this nagging feeling that they're pushing me too hard to get the contract signed. I know that's silly, it would mean a great deal of money for both of us in the end, but they're pushing me too hard. Like if I don't sign it, then something bad will happen to me. I'm not making any sense, am I?"

"You are actually. I'd not sign it simply because you don't feel right. You've never not trusted your gut. This seems a bad time and a great deal of money to go against it now. Just tell them you've changed your mind. Or I will. As I said, I'd have no trouble doing it for you." Locke said nothing for a few moments, and Zander changed the subject. "You should have read over the one from Demi. It was a no-brainer right from the start. You won't believe how many times they spelled the name of the company wrong."

He realized that he wasn't listening, so he went back to work on the other papers he had on his desk. Knox had dropped off the research that was needed for an upcoming trial he was working on, and he was excited to have all the information. Knox was the best researcher he'd ever met, and they worked well together. He was on his second stack of paperwork from Knox when his phone rang.

With a bark of his last name, he answered the phone. But whoever was on the other end said nothing back. He thought perhaps he might have startled them; he could be a little harsh when he had to answer the phone in his office. Waiting just long enough for the person to have said something, he hung up the phone without another word. He looked at Locke when he said his name.

"I'm not going to do it." Before he could change his mind, he put the contract in the shredder. He loved the sound of it going through the thing and the final noises it made. "Thank you for that. I think I would have gone back and forth on it for days if you hadn't taken it out of my hands. I feel better already."

"That's what I'm here for. The other contract bother you? If so, it can meet the same fate." He said that he actually felt good about that one. "It's ready for you to sign. I have markers for the places you're supposed to sign and then initial. Also, I've marked the place where it says that if the contract is null and void for any reason, I listed the ones that you said, then they'll owe us all the money back plus interest."

He not only signed it where it needed to be, but he also asked for it to be notarized. He was able to do that for him as well. Once it was put in the file where it needed to be, he sent copies of it to the company that he was dealing with, and that was all he had for him. Still, he didn't move out of the room.

"I've been thinking about the hospital." He told him how they'd cut funding to them by sixty-five percent this summer. "Yeah, that's what I'm thinking about. I think that next year the only thing we fund is the Martha Grable Foundation and the new wing. I had Alex go over the paperwork they sent to us about the money that they need for the next year, and she said that they're spending money on things that haven't been approved by the board. I can't remember right off the top of my head all the numbers, but she said that they're spending a lot of money on things like outings for the staff. The only staff who get to go on these things are the directors. Not even doctors are getting to go to make them feel better about working there."

"I can get the real paperwork if you want. I'm

sure whatever they sent you about the funding for those things is way off. They seem to think that we're stupid when it comes to donating money." He agreed. "All right. Let me see what I can find out for you two. Alex is really good at sniffing out money that shouldn't be used. I'd trust her with my money over anyone else touching it. I'll start on it today."

That seemed to be all Locke needed to talk about, so when he stood up to leave, he handed him the second contract copies. They were for his files at his office. They did that in the event that something happened to one or the other offices.

It took him the rest of the morning to finish filing the contracts that they had on file. He would usually bring out copies of the ones that were due for a payment from them to make sure that the company was paying on time. So far, his work pattern was working out well for him, and he had only missed one payment in all the years he'd been keeping track of things for the family. Just after lunch, he was back to work on the paperwork for the trial again.

He didn't usually take on trials that had nothing to do with his family. This one had been different when he'd found out that one of the patients from the hospital was being sued for nonpayment of billing. Mr. Shoe had been making the monthly pre-arranged payments for ten years to pay it off, when all of a sudden, they turned it over for collections.

Now, every day, sometimes as many as five times a day, they'd call him up and hound him for payments. Nearly twice what he'd been paying the hospital when it was still with them. Since he was on a fixed income, he'd had to go without food some weeks just so he could pay the minimum. And even then, they'd hound him for more.

When his phone rang again, he said his name like he would to anyone in his family. There was still no one speaking on the other end of the call. He nearly hung up again when something occurred to him. He whispered slightly in the phone to ask who it was. When he still got nothing, he hung up again. This was just ridiculous, he thought to himself. He didn't have time to see what the hell was going on with the phone calls.

At just before six, his phone having rung five more times without any contact, he was ready to call it a day. He had a secretary, but she'd taken the day off for a doctor's appointment, and he'd had to answer the phones. Not that he usually minded that, but he was going to have to ask her if she got the same sort of calls when she was out front. He also needed to ask her about something else that occurred to him today, and that was the lack of filing cabinets that could be used in an outer office.

Did they need more, or did she have plans to have them delivered already? She usually took care of those things, and he wasn't going to mess her up by ordering more when she'd taken care of it. Brenda was good at her job, and he didn't want to piss her off by stepping on her toes. He knew better.

Going home, he stopped by the post office to pick up his mail. He didn't know why he had a post office box; he got the same mail at home. Deciding to do something about that, he made himself a note on his phone to call about that in the morning. There were three other things on his list of things to do tomorrow, and he was quite pleased with himself that there were only four things on it when there had been fourteen just this morning. Of course, he kept adding and taking away from it as he went today, so it could have been as many as twenty or twenty-five by the time he was finished. He loved taking notes and having them ready when he needed them.

After dinner, he went to his office again to make sure that he didn't forget anything on his desk at home. It was just as neat as the one that he'd left at the office, and he was glad. Taking out his checkbook, Zander paid a few bills that had been due, then he went to the living room to watch a little television. His cell phone rang with the same number as before, and he decided that he wasn't going to answer it.

It rang five more times, him answering it after the second time, so he was pissed off. If this kept up, he was going to have his cell phone number changed as he didn't have time to answer his cell phone anymore than he did the one in his office. Whoever it was, he hoped they were having a good time because all they were doing was pissing him off. He had to set the phone down gently at the end, or he might well have thrown it across the room and been done with it.

Finally, when he went up to bed at ten, he'd had enough of it that he turned off his phone. He knew that his brothers would be worried if they couldn't get in touch with him, so he called Locke to let him know what was going on.

"Have you let it go to voicemail?" He said that he had once, and nothing. They'd not only not left a voicemail, but they also hung on the line for several minutes, saying nothing. "I'd talk to Brenda in the morning and see if she's had any trouble like you said. I can't think of a single reason why someone would call you that many times and not answer you. Perhaps it's some kid that got your number somehow."

"I don't know, but if I find out, I'm going to murder them. It's been driving me crazy all day. I'm afraid to not answer it today because what if it's someone who needs me? Then I get aggravated when no one speaks. Am I that hard to talk to?" Locke said he didn't think so. "I don't know what's going on, but I've had enough. If you need me between now and when I get to work in the morning, send up a smoke signal. I'm not answering my phone."

They both laughed, and Zander felt reasonably better about the whole thing and was able to go to sleep when he got into bed. He hated that he'd come to turning off his phone, but he didn't think he'd get any sleep if he hadn't.

The next morning, he got up and left his phone off. He was having a good morning and didn't want to ruin it before going to work. As he was leaving his house, having told Brenda of the calls, she said that if she had any trouble at home, she'd let him know. But so far, whoever it was wasn't calling the house directly. The only landline he had was in the kitchen and office, but they were two different phone numbers, so he didn't know what to think. Brenda didn't know anything about the calls.

"I've made notes on calls that have come in that were a wrong number before. I would usually keep track of them just so I'd know if it came up again. But no, I've never had any trouble with people calling and not saying anything. If I have any trouble today, I'll let you know." He thanked her and then asked about her appointment. "I'm as healthy as a horse he said. I do hope he meant that in a good way. But my physical went well, and now I'm only waiting on the blood work to come back. I was telling him how you've put that treadmill in the break room, and I've been using it, and he thought that was grand. I told him, too, that the two of us were eating better as well."

"Thanks to Demi being on the kick of using only fresh foods." She laughed and told him that she didn't feel the need to cheat either. "She has my cook fixing me better meals, too. I'm enjoying feeling better all the time, I have to admit. Not that I'd tell Demi and Mandy that. August said that they made fun of him when he told them how much better he was feeling."

"I'll keep it to myself, too, then. I feel great, but I'll act like I'm not the next time they come around. We don't want them to get too big a head about this." After making sure that she knew about his one appointment today, he went into his office.

He loved being an attorney and being able to take on the cases that he wanted to. But what he loved most was helping his family with their legal needs. It also made it so that he could talk to them once a week or more, so that he could catch up on what they were doing with themselves. He dearly loved his family and was glad that they were happily married, too. He was going to be the most beloved uncle when they started having children.

~*~

Knox and Elaine were having fun at the RV show. He'd
found one online and thought it would be the perfect
way for them to see what was out there in the way of
campers. He'd done his research too and knew which
one to buy, but they still wanted to look around and see
what the others had to offer. They were going through
their second rig when one of the salesmen approached
Elaine. He was still in the camper when she stepped
out and stood back to hear what he was saying to her.

"I can get you help if you need it." Elaine
said that she was just fine and was looking with her
husband. "There are laws about spousal abuse. I can
get you away from him if you'd like."

He remembered the bruises to her face about
the time she did and put her hand to her eyes. She told
him she was fine and that it wasn't what it looked like;
she'd been in an accident. He just wouldn't let it go, so
he went to save her from more embarrassment.

The salesperson followed them around for the
next hour. Knox never left her side in all that time and
tried to get her in a better mood. It had taken him all
morning to get her out of the self-conscious mood, and
within one minute, the man had crushed her back to
being afraid of what people would think about her
face.

The bruises weren't so bad now, but they were
still there. Yellowed now with age, she had covered

them up with a little makeup so that she didn't draw attention to herself. He wanted to knock the shit out of the man who was bothering her, but kept his cool. They were moving onto the next group of campers when he grabbed her arm.

"I'm going to have to have you release this woman. She needs help getting away from you." Knox, trying his best to remain calm, told him to back off; he didn't have it right. "I know what you're doing to her. You're to step back. I've called the police."

"For what?" He accused him of beating her. "I am not. She's been hurt, yes, but not by me. If you would have just asked, we would have told you." He heard the sirens just as he was getting ready to move on to another group of campers. "Great. Now we're going to draw more attention to her accident, and you've embarrassed my wife."

"I'd rather be wrong than to allow her to be beaten again by you." Elaine was trying to explain to the man what had happened when the police pulled up in front of them. He knew one of the cops, Captain Waller, from the local police station. The man, he'd never caught his name, told what his side of the story was.

"You all right, Elaine?" She said she was embarrassed. "No doubt you are. I'm sorry about this, but if you were to give me a moment, I'll take care of things here."

"I tried to tell him that I was all right. But he grabbed me and told me to get away from Knox. Like he was the one who hurt me." Waller said that he'd talk to the other man. "I wish you luck. He's not been listening to me at all. Even Knox tried to be nice to him about it."

"Mr. Coulter? That's your name, isn't it?" He said that was his name, and he wanted Knox to be arrested for spousal abuse. "There isn't a more loving couple than these two are. You've got it all wrong."

"I'm not wrong. Just look at her. It looks like he's beaten her up in the last few weeks. I have a sister at home, and I'd hope that someone would make sure she was all right if she were being beaten up." Waller said that she'd been beaten up by the principal at the grade school. "Is that what he told you? He's trying to get out of trouble here, and I want him arrested. No one should be able to knock someone around like he has this woman and get away with it."

"I'm telling you you've got it all wrong. Now calm down a minute and listen to me." Waller told how she'd been hurt and how the man who had done it was in jail. Knox could tell that he still didn't believe it, so he wrapped his arm around Elaine when she looked like she was going to cry. They'd gathered a large group of people around them now, and there were cell phones out recording it. It might well have been funny, but the truth needed to be told. Waller finished the story and looked at him. "This man here has been doing a good job keeping his wife safe since that morning, and you should apologize to them both. You've barked up the wrong tree in this, I'm afraid."

"She'd say anything to save him." Knox rolled his eyes at the other man. "That's the way that it works. She'll get beaten, and then he'll make up to her, and she'll go back to him. It's sick, is what it is."

"Mister, you're starting to piss me off." He lunged at him, and Knox didn't move. "You're a big man, are you? You don't have any idea what you're talking about. We just got married a few weeks ago, and this bruising was there to begin with. She was hurt by David Sheen, the principal at the elementary school."

He was being dragged away by the police, and Elaine stood by him. He could almost feel her embarrassment, and he felt bad for her. When the man was finally gone, they decided to go home, as the trip had been ruined by the man. Taking her to the one camper that he'd done the most research on, he asked her if she wanted it. It took him an hour to show her what it could do to make her feel like she could get into it again.

"If we get it today, we still have plenty of time

to take it out before winter sets in. It has an all-season furnace/air conditioner too, so we'd have heat. It also has that really nice fireplace, too, that can keep us warm." She asked how long it would take for them to do a shake-down trip. "I'd say about a week. Then we can make a list of things that we need in it when we take it on a more long-distance trip. I've thought about kitchen stuff too, spices and the like. We'll pick them up as we need them. I don't see us cooking much in the camper. I want to see the sites with you."

"So we just pack up some clothing and buy what we feel we need as we go? That sounds like it might be expensive." He said it was going to be their first vacation home together, and they wanted it to be perfect. "I love that idea of not cooking. I don't enjoy it anyway, so that would be something we can mark off our list. I do love that we can have snacks in the big refrigerator plus drinks."

"My truck will pull it easily, and if it doesn't, I was thinking we could get something that matches the camper. We want to look good when we show up at a campground." She laughed, and he could have jumped for joy. "I've been reading up on things that we're going to need, like propane tanks. This one comes with two, so we don't have to worry about running out of hot water or heat if we get this one."

"I love that it has two bedrooms too, and that

one of them is a bunk bed. If we still have it when we have children, it'll be nice for them to have their own space." She ran her hands along the ladder that was hanging along the bunks. "By the time they come along, we'll be old pros at this, don't you think?"

"I think that you're right. I'm thinking that we need to get a bigger truck before then, too. One with four doors so that it'll be easier to get them in and out of." He could tell that she was warming to the idea, and he was too. If they wanted, they could have the tanks filled and be on their way by morning. They'd not go far; it was just a trial period for them, but they'd have fun doing what they wanted when they wanted. "What do you say? Do we buy this one or wait and see others before we decide?"

"I think we should buy this one. Not this model one, right? They'll give us another one so that we can have brand new." He said they'd go over and pick it up at the lot, wherever they said. "I want to go camping so bad. This is going to be so much fun for the two of us."

"You know it." They walked around it more and decided that they couldn't do any better. With the show price, they were getting a great deal on it, too, so they decided to purchase the one that he'd done all the research on. Just as they were going to find a salesman for the area they were in, someone came to find them. It was the boss of the man who had accused him of beating Elaine. "I don't know if I want to deal with this company."

"I don't know either. He was so rude and embarrassed me to death. I knew that I should have stayed home." Then, he pointed out they'd not have the camper of their dreams. "I know, but I've never wanted to hit someone as much as I did him at that moment. The guy was getting on my last nerve with accusing you of hurting me."

"Hello. I'm sorry about what happened before. I've sent him back to the dealership. Is there anything I can do for you to purchase this fine camper?" Knox had dealt with salesmen before and knew that he'd try anything to get them into the one that was the most expensive. Knox asked him what kind of discount he was going to give them for their embarrassment. The man laughed. "I'll give you an extra twenty percent off the sale price above the one that is the show discount. In addition to that, I'll pay for it to be cleaned up at the dealership for you as well as fill the tanks for you."

"Will we be taking this one?" He said no, he had a better model at no extra charge at the dealership that he'd sell to them with all the perks. "If it's better, what can we expect from it?"

"You're a shrewd man. I'll have it cleaned up now, and you and Mrs. Erickson can go right over and have a look at it. If it's not what you want, then I'll sell you this one at a discount more than I've already offered you."

The dealership wasn't that far away, so they made the trip there. The camper was still being cleaned up, so they took a look at the things they might need to go camping. There were plugs and cords that he had read about, but nothing he knew how to make work. They might have to have their shake down in the yard before he'd feel comfortable enough to go out into the wild, so to speak, and try his hand at camping. They were going to need to have several shake downs if he had to figure it out in one trip.

"Mr. Erickson?" He said that was him to the salesperson on the floor. "Mr. Claude said to put everything you're going to need in the camper. So you don't have to purchase any of this for your trip."

"I'm not even sure what any of this stuff is. We're going to be new to camping." He told him that they'd do fine and to watch some videos on the internet, and they'd get it sooner rather than later. "I hope so. This has been a dream of ours for a while now. We're hoping to see the country inside this thing."

"I'm supposed to tell you that the rig is a bit longer than the one at the show. It has not just bunk beds in the back of it, but there is an office of sorts, too, that can be hooked up to the internet when you have it. Also, you might want to know that there is a coupon for a discount on internet service if you need it." He told the man that they would. "I figured as much. It's about ready for you to have a look at. You're getting one hell of a deal if you don't mind me saying so."

"I'm glad to hear that." The camper was longer than the one that they'd seen at the show. Not only that, but it was all fresh too, like the cleaning they'd done had taken out all the new smells and made it seem like a home. As they inspected the camper, they talked about how much fun they were going to have when they went out, and he was happy that she was in such a better mood. He loved his wife with all his heart.

As soon as they got home, having eaten dinner in town, they started looking at videos on the links that the salesman, Danny, had given them. It was a little daunting knowing all the things that they had to do, but they were going to do it. As soon as they were ready for bed, all the things they'd learned buzzing in their head, they talked for a while as they lay there.

"It's going to be fun once we get it down." He agreed with Elaine and told her they had a lot to learn. "We should just camp in it in the yard a couple of times so that we know how to hook things up. At the very least until we know what we're doing."

He agreed with her. "I think we'll get it down easily enough. It's just a bit overwhelming now." He hoped so anyway. "In a few months, less I'm betting we'll wonder what all the fuss was about."

"I hope so." As they went to sleep, he held her in his arms. There was a lot to learn, but they were both smart and knew how to ask for help when they needed it. As soon as he felt himself drifting off, he thought of how much fun they were going to have when the children came around. He hoped it was soon, but didn't care. So long as they were together and happy, he was going to take things as they came to them.

Before You Go...

HELP AN AUTHOR

write a review

THANK YOU!

Share your voice and help guide other readers to these wonderful books. Even if it's only a line or two, your reviews help readers discover the author's books so they can continue creating stories that you'll love. Log in to your favorite retailer and leave a review. Thank you.

AWARD WINNING, BESTSELLING AUTHOR

Kathi S. Barton is an award-winning and bestselling author known for her steamy paranormal romances and unforgettable characters. A recipient of the prestigious Pinnacle Book Achievement Award, her books have topped the charts on Amazon and All Romance eBooks, earning her a loyal global readership.

Kathi lives in Nashport, Ohio, with her husband, Paul. When she's not crafting passionate love stories set in magical worlds, she enjoys camping, exploring local auctions, and attending county fairs, where Paul showcases his artwork and pottery. Her creative spark — fueled by a muse she describes as a cross between Jimmy Stewart and Hugh Jackman — brings her stories to vivid, heartfelt life.

Paranormal romance with plenty of heat is her favorite genre, and she loves connecting with her readers. Feel free to reach out — Kathi would love to hear from you.

Email: aaronskiss@gmail.com

Follow Kathi on her blog: http://kathisbartonauthor.blogspot.com/

www.ingramcontent.com/pod-product-compliance
Lightning Source LLC
Chambersburg PA
CBHW020752210626
46807CB00018B/2528